Cat "Tails" to Soothe the Soul

By
Diane Dippelhofer

PublishAmerica
Baltimore

First printing

ISBN: 1-4137-5841-X
PUBLISHED BY PUBLISHAMERICA, LLLP
www.publishamerica.com
Baltimore

Printed in the United States of America

This book is dedicated to all the organizations that care for, protect, and support the orphaned, helpless, and lost animals in the world; and to all animal lovers who cherish the special gifts their pets bestow upon them and reciprocate by caring for them responsibly and *always* with love.

A special dedication goes to Faygo, Skunk, Baby, Caesar, Tabitha, Rocky, Patches, and Maggie. My world has been a better place because of them.

Acknowledgments

Cats have been a part of my life since childhood. They've put smiles on my face when there were frowns, laughter in my voice when there were tears, and peace when there was turmoil. Without them there would have been no stories to write.

Many thanks go to Jean, Tina, Carla, and Carol for encouraging me to pursue my dream. To Carol Harlow and Joe Dusza I owe a debt of gratitude for their willingness to be my "readers" and to offer constructive criticism when this effort was in its infancy.

A special thanks to Carol Creeger who fit me into her busy schedule and photographed me for the back cover.

My husband, Joe, deserves a medal for his patience. Instead of complaining whenever my writing cut into our time together, he understood my obsessive need and nudged me along. Just like the cats, he taught me valuable lessons in life and love.

I mustn't forget to give credit to Maggie, my tiger cat. With a sharp meow and a swipe of her paw, she set me straight on the cat's point of view in the stories. I think they're better because of her.

If man could be
Crossed with a cat,
It would improve man
But deteriorate the cat.

– Mark Twain

CONTENTS

Preface   9

The Gift of Hope   11

Taking a Chance   21

The Four-Legged Professor   26

Unconditional Love   44

A Nosy Solution   53

The Purrfect Choice   73

The Cat's Pledge   79

Preface

I was still in diapers when I became a cat lover, and my fascination with them has never waned.

They've taught me about love, patience, and understanding. Their intense concentration and excitement when toying with an ant or swatting a dandelion remind me that the blessings of nature include the small wonders, too.

When my cat shuns the sixty-dollar play station to chase sunbeams across the carpet floor, I realize the latest and greatest gadgets aren't required to be happy or satisfied.

The days when I'm racing around like a wild woman bent on accomplishing all my daily commitments, and I happen to notice Maggie lounging lazily on the bed, I sometimes get the urge to yank her off her cushy pillow. But then she raises her head, yawns, and smiles at me, and my resentment at her obliviousness to my complicated life vanishes as she reminds once again that it's OK to take a break.

And finally, by respecting their independence and individual quirks, and forgiving them their irritating habits, I've become more accepting of others by remembering that everyone brings some unique gifts to the human race.

The following stories and their messages were inspired by these furry four-legged felines. I hope you enjoy them as much as I enjoyed writing them.

The Gift of Hope

"Forty-eight, forty-nine, fifty." Matt looked at the white pills lined up like soldiers in formation on the end table. He put the lid on the empty pill bottle and walked through the kitchen and onto the back porch where several trash bags were neatly stacked. Opening the nearest one, he dropped the pill bottle in and retied the bag.

"Better put down some salt," he muttered. "No sense in someone breaking a leg when they carry me out."

After sprinkling the icy steps and walkway, he went inside and thoroughly inspected each room. He wanted nothing left for others to do. The rooms were spotless from yesterday's cleaning except for some ground-in dirt on the entry hall carpet.

The new owners, a young couple whose house was destroyed by a fire, could move in as soon as they were notified. He wished he'd known of their tragedy before telling the Salvation Army to pick up his furnishings. He'd only kept the bare necessities: a mattress and bed linens, an easy chair, lamp, end table, one set of dishes and silverware, and a set of towels.

Returning to the kitchen, Matt opened the top drawer next to the sink and pulled out two thick envelopes. "Last Will and Testament" was clearly written on the one. He reread the one addressed to Ron Stiple, his attorney. Confident Ron would understand his instructions, he licked both envelopes and set them on the clean counter.

After filling his glass with water, he went to the living room and sat in his chair, setting the glass next to the pills. He pulled his reading glasses from the pocket of his flannel shirt and adjusted them on his nose. Reaching over, he picked up the photo album from the floor and looked at the picture on the cover.

Tears sprang to his eyes. Their wedding day. "We were so young, Mary. But we went ahead and did it anyway. We proved our parents wrong, didn't we?" *Had thirty years really gone by?* Mary's words, spoken every year on their anniversary, reverberated through his mind: "Sometimes I feel like we've been married forever, but at the same time it feels like we're still on our honeymoon."

He studied the photo of the two of them together, their eyes sparkling with anticipation of their future together. With her long, golden hair and deep-blue eyes, and his dark hair and eyes, their friends had dubbed them Barbie and Ken. She looked like a fragile princess in her white wedding gown with its pearl-covered bodice. At twenty, they'd both been so naïve, but firm in their commitment to each other.

After gently caressing the picture he opened the album and began turning the pages. He was glad she'd ignored his complaints about the excessive amount of pictures that she'd always insisted on taking. In the three months she'd been gone they'd acted as a conduit for him to talk to her. Each picture triggered a memory. He paused at the one of Mary lying on a bear rug.

"That was quite a honeymoon, wasn't it?" He straightened his legs out and rested his head against the plush backrest, letting his thoughts relive it.

"What happened?" Mary shouted when the room was suddenly thrown into darkness.

"It's OK, honey. The storm must've knocked the power lines down."

"But what'll we do? We'll freeze to death without any heat."

"It'll be all right," he said, wrapping his arms around her. He rubbed her back until he felt her muscles relax. "I'm going out to the porch and bring in some firewood. This cabin's so small the fire will heat it up in no time. Will you be all right?"

"Yes," she whimpered. "I'm sorry for being such a baby. When I was a kid we went without power for a week during an ice storm. My dad was out of town at the time. We lived out in the country without any neighbors close by. My mom didn't know what to do. It was terrible."

"Don't worry. I'll take care of you," he said, cupping her face with his hand.

"You make me feel so safe."

"We lived on love those three days." He chuckled, remembering that because they were unable to navigate their car through the drifts, they'd had to ration their meager and odd assortment of snacks – wine, cheese, animal crackers, popcorn, Snickers and Reese's Peanut Butter Cups while they were snowed in. Instead of letting the weather ruin their honeymoon, they'd taken advantage of the solitude and spent hours talking of their future together. He'd listened as Mary shared her dreams, delighting in her childlike enthusiasm for life, and vowed to let nothing erase it.

For thirty years he'd never tired of taking care of her. His hardest challenge was controlling her overactive imagination. He'd often told her, "Your picture should be next to the word 'worrier' in the dictionary." He'd learned that whenever she was stressed her right eye twitched uncontrollably. It was time then to pat her head and say, "Give your mind a rest."

He'd quietly listen to her fears and support her decisions. When nothing else relieved her stress, he'd wrap his arms solidly around her, trying to transmit his strength to her. But nothing he did had kept her safe from the monster that had taken her from him.

He forced down the anger brewing beneath the surface like a boiling caldron and glanced at the pills. "Not much longer," he murmured before focusing his attention back to the album.

I'd forgotten we kept this one. It was a picture of their house. Mary'd taken it the day they'd moved in. *It was just about this time of year*, he remembered, noticing the Christmas wreath hung on the front door.

"We sure did a lot of work on this place. Boy, if these walls could talk." Smiling, he looked around, his thoughts replaying the summer day they'd painted this room.

"It's a good thing I covered the entire carpet with plastic. You're the messiest painter I've ever seen."

"I warned you," Mary laughed, rubbing her hand across her once green

T-shirt, now covered with streaks of white. "It looks like you haven't even dipped your brush yet. You're spotless. You could've worn a tuxedo."

"We'll probably need another gallon of paint to replace the gallon in your hair and on your clothes," he joked.

"Well," she said, with a glint of deviltry in her eyes, "as long as we're buying more, we can waste some of this."

Before he could react, she ran her saturated roller down his front.

Matt retaliated with a swipe of his brush across her face. Globs of paint splattered around the room like giant Rorschach inkspots. Jumping back to escape her reach, Matt stepped into the paint can, toppling it over. The cascading liquid slowly crept across the plastic. He slipped on the slick surface and grabbed Mary, pulling her down on top of him. Squeals of laughter rocked the house.

The next day Rev. Clawson told the congregation, "The secret to a happy marriage is working together and making it fun. If you need any hints on how to do that, talk to Mary and Matt." After the service he confessed that he'd witnessed the whole scene through their large picture window when he'd come to visit. Not wanting to disturb them, he'd left without ringing the bell.

Suddenly the ringing of the phone broke the silence. Matt ignored it. "I know I told the phone company to disconnect that." He shrugged. "Nothing I can do about it today. They don't work on holidays."

The distraction caused him to lose his place, so he flipped back a few pages until he saw the picture of a black and gray striped cat.

"Oh, Mary, remember Rover? Bet we had the only cats in the country with dog names." He'd laughed when she'd explained her rationalization by saying, "I went to the Humane Society to get a dog, but this cat looked so pitiful. Since you like them so much, I figured as long as we can name him Rover, I can pretend he's a dog." And from that day on any cat they adopted acquired a name more suited for a dog. Despite her affection for dogs, since adopting Rover, she'd become a staunch cat lover, immediately falling in love with their independent yet loving nature. Over the years whenever she went back to the Humane Society to adopt another animal, she'd always return with a kitten instead of a puppy.

Wearily, Matt stood up and went to the window that looked out over their front yard. Through the gently falling snow he searched for the small cross under the evergreen tree where he'd buried Fido a month ago. Mary would've been devastated to know he was gone. He'd been her shadow, a constant presence by her side during the last months of her life. When the pain woke her, only his steady purring seemed to soothe her.

They'd transferred the nurturing and love they'd stored up for the child they'd never been able to conceive to their cats – and each other. Now he had no one. It made it simple to leave.

The faint sounds of "Silent Night" drew his attention to the house across the street. Carolers stood, bathed in the blinking blue, white, and green Christmas lights strung across the porch. He quickly drew the blinds and turned off the lamp, hoping to dissuade them from stopping as they worked their way through the neighborhood.

Sitting down, he slumped over like a hunchback remembering how Mary and he would welcome the carolers in for hot chocolate and pumpkin bread. He had about an hour to wait before they finished this block. No problem. He didn't need light for the next section. The pictures of their vacation were branded in his mind from the countless hours he'd spent looking at them. They brought him the most comfort, and at the same time, the most pain.

Each year he'd spent months happily planning their next vacation, and each summer his efforts were rewarded by Mary's childlike squeals of joy on every stop they made. They'd visited the usual tourist traps, but their fondest trips were those of the scenic, less-traveled locations. The charm of the locals and the unexpected discoveries were like priceless trinkets they'd talked about for years.

Resting his head against the chair, he closed his eyes and let the memories rush back. His mind became a movie reel, a kaleidoscope of scenes that captured their travels that had covered all fifty states. When he came to their Hawaiian trip, he rose and made his way carefully to the kitchen and over to the nightlight above the counter. He shuffled through the pages until he came to an 8" x 10" picture. Pulling it from its protective sheathing, he studied it for several minutes before returning to his chair. Clutching it tightly he let the memory of that day wash over him.

Their twenty-fifth wedding anniversary. The aqua-blue waters gently lapping the white sands of Kaanapali Beach at sunrise. Mary in a form-fitting flowered muumuu slit discreetly up the side, and he in a matching shirt. Barefooted and holding hands with sweet-scented pink, rose, peach, and white leis around their necks. A stocky Hawaiian standing in front of them. Renewing their vows they'd written themselves. In unison they looked at each other and said, "Like the dawn of this new day, for us it'll be the dawn of another twenty-five years together."

But they'd only had five. His heart felt like it had been burned by a hot poker. "It's not fair," he shouted. "Why? Why? Why?" he moaned, slamming his head back in time to his question before wilting against the cushions, letting his arms hang loosely over the sides.

The darkness acted like a cocoon, wrapping him in his pain. Finally he forced himself to continue. No longer able to hear the carolers, he decided it was safe to turn the light back on. Reopening the album, Mary's bald head stared back at him. He doubled over like he'd been sucker-punched. The devastation of the last year came roaring back. The blood tests. X-rays. More tests. Surgery. The nauseating chemo. The death sentence. And finally, only morphine to dull her pain as the monster unmercifully feasted on her body.

He gasped for breath in between his deep, wracking sobs. As the well of tears ran dry, he rubbed his eyes. The frown between his eyebrows deepened and looked like fissures in the earth as he looked at the photo once more.

"Oh my poor Mary," he said, gently tracing the outline of her bare head with his finger and remembering the first morning he'd woken to see clumps of her blonde hair lying on the pillow. Shock. Sorrow. Pity. Love. Always love.

Once she'd made the decision to shave her head, they'd tackled it like most things—as a team. Wrapped in her favorite fleece robe he'd carried her to the kitchen chair. She'd turned on the electric razor and handed it to him with a nod of her head. Carefully, he'd finished the job the chemo had started.

Choking back a sob, he turned to the last page. "How could I have forgotten that?" he murmured.

Two days after her "behairing" as Mary termed it, she'd come in from the garage with a tray of water paints and brushes and said, "We're painting a collage." Her only stipulation was that neither one could cry.

16

Three hours and much reminiscing later, her head was completely covered with a multitude of words and pictures in every color of the rainbow, depicting their most precious feelings and memories.

Sighing, he rolled his head in a circle to alleviate the kink in his neck and closed the album. The rest of it contained only blank pages. Never to be filled. *Like my life*, he thought. *I can't picture anything, Mary. Since you left, it's like rowing a boat with only one oar. Going in circles with no direction.*

He shook his head as if responding to her. "Hopefully God will forgive me and send me back to you."

Carefully pulling their wedding picture off the cover, he placed it next to the pills. His eyes never left her face as he picked up the first pill, put it in his mouth, and took a sip of water. He reached for the next one.

Suddenly the doorbell broke the silence. Once. Twice. Three times he let it ring, hoping whoever was there would give up and leave.

"Matt. Are you there?"

Jimmy.

"I know you're in there. I see your light on. I've got something for you, and I can't leave it out here."

Knowing the eight-year-old would only leave to bring back his mother, or worse the whole neighborhood, to check on him, he got up and opened the door.

"What's up, champ?" He projected a note of enthusiasm he didn't feel.

"Here's a present for you," Jimmy said, holding out a wicker basket with a red and green checked blanket covering the contents.

"What is it?"

Before Jimmy could answer, a tiny orange and white head popped out from beneath the blanket. It looked up at Matt and let out a high-pitched meow.

"Oh, Jimmy. I can't take this."

"Why not?"

"Well, it's just that…"

"It's all alone. Its mother was killed. The Humane Society said they had no room and were going to put it down, but I told them I knew someone who'd take real good care of it."

17

Jimmy scooted past Matt and set the basket down in the middle of the room.

The tiny creature stumbled over the top and, on shaky legs, staggered over to Matt. Using its needle-sharp claws, it began climbing up his jeans. Grimacing from the razor-like pokes, he reached down and gently pulled it off.

He held it up to his face. "You're mighty spunky for as little as you are."

The kitten batted Matt's nose with its paw before licking it with its pink, sandpapery tongue. It meowed once and began purring.

"She likes you, Matt," Jimmy shouted.

"She's a cutie. I appreciate you thinking of me, but I can't accept your gift. Why don't you keep it?"

"Oh, it's not from me."

"What? Then who's it from?"

"Oh, I almost forgot." Jumping up, Jimmy ran out the front door and disappeared. Seconds later he returned with his arms full of presents. "When I told everybody you were getting a kitten, they bought these for you. We knew you gave away all of Fido's things. There's kitty litter, a litter box, toys. You name it, it's here."

Matt stood there speechless.

"Well, I've got to go. We're going to midnight mass." Running over to him, Jimmy wrapped his arms around Matt's legs. "Merry Christmas. Mom and I'll be over tomorrow."

"But wait." Before Matt could stop him, the youngster ran out the door.

He looked at the kitten that was licking his hand. "I can't keep you. I just can't. Believe me, it's for the best." Kneeling down, he drew back the blanket to put it back but stopped when he noticed a card on the bottom. Setting the kitten on the floor, he opened it.

"Mary," he gasped, recognizing the smiley faces she'd dotted her "I's" with.

Joy shot through his body like internal fireworks. His eyes bounced haphazardly off the words. Trying to focus, he inhaled deeply. The scent of Obsession, Mary's favorite cologne, drifted up. Calmer, he read her message:

My Most Wonderful Matt,

I know you're hurting and you're questioning why our time together was cut short. I don't have an answer to that, but I do know it's time for you to start living again. So get off your ass, put a smile on that handsome face, and do something silly – just like we used to.

I was so thankful to be blessed with a man who shared his love so selflessly. Now it's time for you to share with someone else.

You can start with that bundle of fur. She needs someone who can give her love, strength, and wisdom as she explores life. Her name is Hope, for hope is the most powerful gift we can give each other.

Love forever and beyond,
Mary

The pale green card was dotted with tears by the time he finished reading. *So this is what you and Jimmy were talking about.*

A week before she'd died, Mary told him to bring Jimmy to see her. Despite his protests that the child would wear her out, she'd insisted. It was the only time during her battle that she'd demanded anything. He couldn't refuse, but he'd hovered outside the closed bedroom door, worried about the drain Jimmy's visit would have on her. All he'd heard, however, were soft murmuring and a few giggles.

Afterwards she'd seemed more at peace, and he'd seen that telltale twinkle in her eyes that meant she was keeping a secret from him. When he'd asked her about it, she'd replied, "You'll find out at the right time."

He reread her note. "You knew me so well."

Wiping the tears from his cheeks, he walked over to the table, scooped up the pills and placed the card in their place.

"MEOWWW!"

Startled at the kitten's screech, he spun around, dropping the pills. They scattered across the carpet like pellets shot from a BB gun.

"Where are you, Hope?" He dropped to his knees and searched through the torn wrapping paper, boxes, and gift bags. Out of the corner of his eye he saw a streak of orange and white batting one of the pills like it was an ant.

Wedging it into the corner, Hope picked it up in her mouth.

"Stop," he screamed and lunged across the room to grab her. Quickly he gently squeezed the sides of her tiny mouth open. Using his finger, he flicked the pill out.

Her deep blue eyes crinkled shut as she meowed softly.

"I know you're upset. But that's not food. In fact," he said, looking around, "I better pick the rest of these up before you get any more ideas."

He emptied out the largest box and placed the blanket from the basket in the bottom before putting her in it. Twenty minutes later he heard her whining.

"Just a minute. Forty-eight, forty-nine. OK. That's all of them." He dropped them into one of the empty gift bags and carried it outside, placing it on top of the nearest garbage bag.

Stepping back inside, he tiptoed into the living room and looked into the box where he'd left her. She looked up at him expectantly. Leaning over, he lifted her and sat her on the floor.

"Well, Hope, I guess it's just you and me now. I bet you're hungry, and I don't even have milk for you."

On wobbly legs, Hope walked over to a red and gold bag and climbed in. The bag came alive as the kitten bounced around inside. Suddenly her head shot out with a packet of evaporated milk in her mouth.

Grinning, Matt said, "I guess we'll help each other. Is that OK?"

"Meoowwww."

Taking a Chance

I've been on Death Row for five years. Today I'm getting out – no matter what. The door to our cellblock opened and our guard entered. Sally, who could've passed for a pro football linebacker, was blocking my view of the visitor she was talking to. As they came closer, I stood at attention with an angelic look pasted on my face, waiting to spring into action.

I heard the stranger say, "Isn't this one adorable?"

"Yes, Mrs. Gurney," Sally replied. "The Humane Society has several kittens, but we have a really sweet, older cat, Rocky, that's already declawed and castrated."

"I want a kitten," the woman said firmly.

Shooting me a look of pity, Sally unlocked the door to one of my competitors' cages and picked up a tiny white ball of fur. "I'll take you and Snowball to the play room to get acquainted, and you can decide whether she's right for you."

I jumped onto the bars of my cage and let out a yowl. "Wait! Look at me." The door slammed shut on my plea. "I don't get it. Snowball poops in her feed bowl, and Gurney swoons in delight. Yesterday Blackie peed in his water bowl and he got adopted. What is it with humans? Are they all fascinated with bodily functions?"

"Quiet, I'm napping," hissed Tinker, my neighbor in the next cell.

"Tough." Jumping into my litter box, I used my paws like shovels and sprayed the litter and its deposits in her direction.

"Hey. I just took a bath. Now I've got to wash again thanks to you."

"Sorry," I said grudgingly, "but you'll understand my frustration when you've been here longer." I paced back and forth continuing my diatribe. "My nine lives are running out. Why won't anyone pick me? I'm low maintenance. I don't throw up hairballs like those long-haired Persians, and I'll eat anything. Those finicky purebreds cost a fortune to feed."

My meows jumped an octave as my frustration grew, and I swiped at the ball in my cage, ducking when it boomeranged off the bars. "And I'm cheap. Just give me a crumpled up piece of paper to play with and I'm content. I don't need fancy toys with feathers or catnip. Or those hoity-toity carpeted condos."

I sat down only to spring up as I remembered a few more of my virtues. "Plus, for the last two years no one's broken my sharp shooting record for hitting the litter box. And I wouldn't get on the kitchen counters. Well…at least not when they're looking."

"Humans need to feel needed. Kittens are like babies. Helpless."

Tinker's words of wisdom did nothing to placate me. "If humans only understood Kitty-Kat. I'd tell them how smart older cats are compared to sniveling kittens that can't find their way out of a paper sack."

"You know, Rocky, you're part of the problem."

"What?" I howled.

"Since I've been here I've seen you blow your chances twice. That farmer—"

"That grouchy old geezer. All he wanted was a mouse catcher. No way was I living in a dirty, smelly old barn."

"How about that lady last week? She was nice and definitely interested until you nipped her in the ankle."

"Yeah." I laughed. "I really had to think fast when she started talking about her rugrats. No thanks. I want to keep my tail and eyes. No kid's going to dress me up in doll clothes and push me around in a baby carriage."

"They won't keep you here forever."

I winced at her reminder. Flopping down on the carpet remnant, I ran through my rules for an owner and decided I wasn't being too rigid: energetic enough to play with, smart enough to know when to leave me alone, and most importantly—

The door suddenly opened, and I waited to hear Snowball's fate.

"I'm sure we have another one you'll like better."

I've still got a chance! I lunged onto the bars of the cage. Their conversation ceased when I let out an ear splitting "Meeeooowwwww."

"What in the world?" I saw Gurney's feet head in my direction.

I coaxed her closer by emitting high-pitched squeaks.

"Are you hurt, dear?" Gurney asked, bending over and looking in my cage.

Yipes. I let out a hiss as loud as a cougar's and stood, puffing my fur out like a lion's mane.

"My goodness," she said, jumping back.

Sally glared daggers at me and said, "I'm so sorry. He's usually so sweet. Something must've scared him."

You got that right. Sally led her away. I heard their muffled talking, interspersed with several "just darlings." The squeaking of metal signaled another victim had been plucked from its cage. I heard their footsteps leave the room.

"Have you totally lost your mind?" Tinker shouted. "You had her. Then you turned psycho. You must have a death wish. I can't believe —"

"But did you see her? She's a dinosaur."

"She's no older than Sally's grandmother, Mrs. Burnett."

"Right," I said sarcastically. "She's got enough wrinkles to be an accordion."

"Well, she moved pretty fast when she thought you were hurt. I think she's kinda cool with her sneakers and jogging suit instead of those dusters and orthopedic shoes that Burnett wears."

"I still say she's too old and probably has enough trouble caring for herself let alone a cat. Nope. My owner's gotta be young enough to outlive me. I've no intention of coming back here."

"After your Freddy Krueger impression I don't think you'll have to worry about her picking you," Tinker snickered.

Before I could comment the door opened. "I'm sorry, Mrs. Gurney. I'm afraid Bitsy has a temper."

I giggled. *Bitsy hooked another one,* I thought, as I saw Gurney suck her finger. I choked on my laughter when Sally said, "Rocky would never scratch because he's been declawed." Hurrying over, Sally unlatched my door and motioned Gurney over.

As soon as the old lady squatted in front of the cage I hissed at her and threw in a deep growl. Instead of backing away, however, she sat down and stared silently at me for several seconds.

"He looks just like the first cat my husband and I adopted forty-five years ago. Right after our only child died from leukemia. Roy thought it would help me fill that void. That's why I came today."

She paused for a minute. When she spoke again her voice sounded as if she was trying to expel a hairball from her throat. "I just lost Roy two months ago. The house is so empty." A mournful sound of a half laugh, half cry, escaped her. "He always said I needed someone to fawn over or I wasn't happy. Now I have no one."

My rules melted away like snow on a warm, spring day.

She pursed her lips together and sat up straighter. "That's why I want a kitten. I don't want to bury another soul. I want to be the first to go this time." She looked at me sadly. "Sorry. You're as handsome and feisty as Cleo was, but you're too old."

She started to push herself up, but I leaped forward, pushed open the unlatched door, and jumped into her lap. Standing on my hind legs, I snuggled my paws between the layers of double chins around her neck and stared into her eyes.

Pick me. Please. I know what it's like to be lonely. I'll stay with you. I willed my eyes to speak the words I knew she wouldn't understand.

"Oh, you're a lover, too, aren't you? But I can't do it." Her voice cracked as she put her hands around my middle to lift me off. I clung to her neck like a drowning person to a lifeline.

She shut her eyes tightly, her wrinkles framing them like riverbeds, their banks overflowing with her tears.

Don't cry, I purred, patting her cheek with my paw. I rubbed her nose with mine and revved my engine even more. She must have won the fight with whatever demons she'd been battling because when she opened her eyes they sparkled – not from tears – but like a dirty window that's been washed clean in the sun.

"I'll take him," she said, nodding. She stood up and slung me over her shoulder like a baby and began patting my back as if I should burp.

"I know what you're thinking," I said to Tinker who stood with her tongue hanging out of her open mouth. "Tough. Heck, I'll even wear a baby bonnet."

As she carried me out to the door to freedom, I meowed, "See you on the outside."

When we got to her car she set me gently on the passenger seat, stroked my back, and said, "If you don't mind, I'd like to call you, Chance."

I meowed, "That'd be purrrfect."

The Four-Legged Professor

"Can't you just lift your legs?" Cindy whined.

"It hurts." Seventy-five-year-old Mrs. Shannon suddenly gasped in pain when the nurse jerked her arthritic legs up.

"You're not the only one who's sore. And tired. And fed up." Cindy threw the sheet under the woman's legs and then dropped them with a thud. Walking around the bed, Cindy looked up to see Kris, her supervisor, standing in the doorway.

"When you're done here come to my office." Her tone left no room for argument.

Twenty minutes later Cindy marched in and went over to Kris' desk. Before Kris could speak, she dropped a letter on it. "I'll do us both a favor and tender my resignation."

Her boss sat calmly studying her. Several seconds passed in silence. Deciding Kris wasn't going to waste her breath berating her, Cindy turned to leave. "I'll empty out my locker on my way out."

"I never said I accepted your resignation."

Shocked by Kris' matter-of-fact tone, Cindy whipped around and looked for signs of sarcasm in her eyes, but saw none. "I don't understand. My actions were despicable. Bordering on abusive."

"You're right."

"Then why…?"

"You're the best nurse I've had in my six years as a supervisor."

Cindy gaped at her boss.

"Well, maybe not the best today," Kris said, standing and walking around

26

her desk. She sat down in one of the chairs in front of it and pointed to the chair next to her, indicating for Cindy to sit. "But the point is, you realize your behavior was unacceptable and took responsibility for your actions. That tells me a lot about you."

"Yeah, that I don't belong in this profession."

"No. It tells me you're human." Kris reached over and took Cindy's hand. "I'm not condoning your behavior. But I should've seen it coming. You know, I have to take some of the blame for this."

Cindy frowned in confusion. "You've lost me."

"When I didn't see that energetic, caring young lady I hired five years ago, I should've asked what was wrong, but I thought you'd work through it. I take the blame for that." Kris leaned closer. "But now I'm asking. What's the problem?"

Sighing, Cindy said, "I don't know. I'm just…just…"

"Burnt-out?" Kris asked quietly.

"Yes." Cindy grabbed at the diagnosis like a marathon runner sucking in air. "I have to drag myself to work, and when I'm here, I resent the very people I'm trained to help." Disgusted, she stood up and paced around the room, her arms swinging in the air as she tried to express herself. "I feel like parasites have eaten up all my empathy, leaving me with only frustration and resentment."

Frowning, she massaged her temples. "I can't believe how cruel I was today. I've got no right to be here. When I became a nurse I did it for what I thought were all the right reasons." Like a politician trying to convince her constituents, she ticked them off on her fingers. "I like people. Wanted to take care of those hurting. I couldn't wait to put my skills to use."

Tears glimmered in her eyes. "But all I'm doing lately is making the patients feel worse. It's better if I quit before I really do some harm." She snapped her chin down to emphasize her decision. "You can't possibly want me working here. I've lost it." She fell into the chair and slouched, dropping her head.

Kris watched her for a minute before placing her hand on the distraught woman's arm. "I almost quit nursing."

Shocked, Cindy's dark hair flew over her shoulders as she threw her head back. "You? No way. You've got the best reputation in the county.

Everyone respects you. That's the reason I accepted the job here at Briarwood."

"It's true. I listen to you and it's like hearing myself seven years ago."

"You were burnt-out, too?"

"Like a missile veering off course waiting to crash."

"But you're so together. I can't imagine you ever shouting at a patient, let alone manhandling one." Cindy cringed when she thought of poor Mrs. Shannon. "What did you do to snap out of it?" She sat down again and leaned forward, her eyes pleading for her supervisor to supply the answer she'd been unable to find for weeks.

"I'm not going to answer that. Instead I'm going to put your letter here," Kris said, placing it in a red folder on her credenza. "I want you to agree to put your resignation on hold for a week." She raised her hand to stop Cindy's objection. "You won't be doing your normal duties. I'm giving you another assignment. Let's call it continuing education."

"I still don't understand."

"You just told me you respected me. Will you trust me enough not to question me?"

Cindy nodded.

"Good." Kris quickly jotted something down on her notepad and handed it to Cindy. "I want you to take the rest of today off and relax this weekend. Report here on Monday," she said, pointing to the address she'd written. "Ask for Beth. She'll be expecting you. If you still feel the same in a week as you do now, I'll gladly accept your resignation. However, if you've found the answer to your question, come in here before you start your rounds and remove the letter. You can start fresh, and we'll consider your week off here as time well spent."

Before Cindy could change her mind, Kris got up and walked to the door, turning to give her an encouraging smile. *I leave her in your capable hands, Roscoe,* Kris thought, as she walked from her office.

Monday morning Cindy turned off the busy highway onto a winding drive lined with large oak trees. Reaching the end, she pulled into the parking lot in front of a well-kept, one-story, white building. Turning the car off, she studied the T-shaped building. Mature evergreens towered over it, but the lavender lilac bushes and wildflowers scattered among them created a cozy setting.

Locking her car, she walked to the entrance and took a deep breath to steady her nerves before entering the lobby.

"Hello. You must be Cindy." A dark-haired woman in her mid-forties with a smile that showed a set of white teeth came out from behind the counter. "I'm Beth." Barely coming up to Cindy's shoulders and with a petite build to match her size, she had a surprisingly firm handshake. "We're glad you're here."

"I'm sure Kris told you what happened," Cindy said, lowering her eyes and blushing in embarrassment.

"No. But when someone is sent here to work with Roscoe we know why." Looking down the hall, she said, "Here he comes now."

Cindy followed the woman's gaze, but only saw an odd-looking cat walking towards them. His gait reminded her of a bowlegged football player's.

"What's a cat doing here?"

Beth laughed. "I guess Kris didn't tell you about Roscoe. Well, honey," she said, patting Cindy's arm, "you're in for a real treat."

"Good morning, Roscoe," Beth said, bending over when he lifted his head for her to scratch under his chin. "I want you to meet Cindy. She's going to be working with you."

What on earth was Kris thinking? Was this her way of paying me back? Telling me a mongrel that looks like a poster cat for the Humane Society is a better nurse than I am?

"Come here," Beth said, pulling the reluctant Cindy by her arm, "and meet Roscoe. He's the best nurse we have."

Cindy looked at the homely cat that'd parked at her feet. He looked like two cats combined into one. His body was out of proportion with his small head from the long, thick fur that stood out like he was in a constant state of panic. His ivory-white undercoat was almost hidden by the splatters of gray, orange, and tan fur. Looking as if a frustrated painter had thrown a palette of colors onto his back, they mingled together across his back and down his sides. Only his coal-black head and tail were absent of any other color.

But what grabbed her attention was the intense, appraising gaze of his eyes, the color and size of two-carat emeralds. They looked almost human. She saw excitement, curiosity, and pity staring up at her. And something else. But it alluded her.

Suddenly Roscoe blinked and Cindy jumped, startled at the hold he'd had on her. Determined not to show it, she looked at Beth and said, "I think I've wasted my time, and yours, by coming here. I have no idea what Kris was thinking, but –"

"That's right, you don't. But you trusted her, didn't you?"

"Yes, but if I'd known –"

"Then trust her a little longer," Beth said.

Were they making a fool of her? Should she trust Kris? She looked down at Roscoe. *How could this strange looking feline help me?* He sat calmly watching her, closing and reopening his eyes. *Was that a smile?*

His paw tapped her shoe. "Meow."

Exasperated, Cindy threw up her hands in submission. "All right. Although this just seems –"

"I know, crazy," Beth said. "We nurses like specific answers. Put your clinical skills aside for awhile. You're here to learn something else." Her eyes sparkled with excitement. "Enough chatter. Roscoe's patients are waiting." She picked up a pile of patient charts from the counter. "Just consider him your mentor," she said, dismissing Cindy to answer the phone.

Cindy was too shocked to react.

"Meow."

"What? You expect me to follow you?"

"MeeeeeeooooWWW." The cat trotted down the hall, stopping at the second door to look back at Cindy who still hadn't moved. With a twitch of his bushy tail, he meowed again and went into the room.

"Geez. What have I gotten myself into?" she muttered. Shaking her head, she hurried to join him.

Walking into the room, Cindy saw a plump nurse who was obviously agitated. Her tight gray curls were bouncing like yo-yos as she explained her problem to Roscoe. "Mrs. Howell's still not eating. It looks like we may have to send her to the hospital." She pointed to the plate of food that was still untouched. "I'm afraid she's given up now that her son, John, and his family moved to Oregon and won't be able to visit. You know how she doted on her only grandchild. Can you do anything?"

Trained professionals asking an animal for help? Is this where all the batty nurses end up? Remembering the trust she put in Kris, Cindy put her doubts aside and backed out of the way to watch. The nurse introduced herself as Robin when she came over to join her.

Jumping onto the end of the bed, Roscoe hopped nimbly over Mrs. Howell's legs, landing next to the tray cart swung across the bed.

"Aren't you going to stop him?" Cindy whispered when Roscoe stepped onto it.

"Shh. Just watch."

What kind of place is this? Cindy waited for the cat to help himself to the scrambled eggs, sausage, and toast. Instead, he barely glanced at the plate and began purring loudly.

The woman, propped in a sitting position by two large pillows, opened her eyes. "Hi, Roscoe." When she lifted her skinny arm to touch his wet nose with her finger, Cindy saw veins that looked like mole tracks beneath the translucent skin. "Don't waste your time on me, sweetie," she said, her voice barely above a whisper.

"Meow."

"I miss them so much. But I don't blame them. John had to go where his job sends him." A tear ran down her cheek. "You understand, don't you?"

"Puurrr. Puuuurrrrrr."

Cindy coughed to cover a laugh when Roscoe picked up a piece of sausage in his mouth and dropped it in Mrs. Howell's lap. The frail woman picked it up and held it out for him, but he turned his head away.

"What? You don't want it? But it's good for you." She set the piece down on the tray. Once again Roscoe picked it up and dropped it in her lap. "Come on, baby," she coaxed, holding it out again. "Eat it."

Roscoe only purred louder.

"You're a stubborn one. Just like my grandson, Ronnie. When he was a baby I'd have to eat a piece before he would." A light glimmered in her eyes. "Would that work with you?"

"Meow." The cat leaned towards her.

"OK." She jabbed another sausage link with her fork and ate it. "Now

31

it's your turn." She held out the piece of sausage for him. "Good boy," she said when Roscoe ate it.

Fifteen minutes later Cindy and Robin left Mrs. Howell to watch TV with Roscoe. Cindy waited while Robin stacked the empty plate on the cart.

"How did Roscoe know to do that?" Cindy asked.

"That's nothing," Robin said, shrugging her shoulders. "Meet me in hallway B tomorrow at eleven if you really want to see something."

On their rounds the next morning Cindy kept one eye on her watch. She had to admit her curiosity was aroused. Promptly at eleven, after situating Mr. Foster in his chair by the window to watch the birds at the feeder, Cindy followed Roscoe down the hall.

When they turned the corner she almost tripped over a young man in his early twenties sitting in a wheelchair. Robin caught her arm before she fell and pulled her into a vacant space along the hallway that was lined with people.

"I thought maybe you decided to default, Roscoe," the man said. "Come on. I'm warmed up and ready to beat your furry ass." He laughed when Roscoe twitched his tail at him.

"That's Ray," Robin said.

Cindy watched him easily maneuver his chair, his muscles bulging beneath his T-shirt, to the end of the hall. "What happened to him?"

"He stepped on a mine in Iraq. He was lucky to have only lost his legs. When they brought him here two months ago from the hospital to recuperate, he was the most bitter, angry patient we've ever had."

She stepped out of line to help a patient find a spot and then returned to her place next to Cindy, continuing where she left off. "He'd planned on becoming a football coach when he got out of the Army. At first we felt sorry for him. We understood why he was so angry, but it sure got old after awhile. He'd lie in bed all day, throw things at any nurse that stepped into his room, and refused to see any visitors. He was so belligerent, we used to draw straws each day to see who'd be the unlucky one assigned to his room."

There were no signs of the angry young man now, however, as he worked his way down the hall giving high-fives to the crowd. Robin nudged Cindy and pointed to Ray who'd stopped to kiss Mrs. Sommer, a widow from room 4A, on the cheek. She laughed. "He's quite the flirt now."

Before Cindy could ask what the banner stretched across the opposite end of the hall was for, she heard a loud "GO," followed by loud cheering and clapping. She leaned out in time to see Ray shoot by with Roscoe galloping next to him.

"Come on, Ray. You can do it," Robin urged from the sidelines. "Yes," she screamed, jumping into the air when Ray, his arms pumping like pistons, propelled the wheelchair through the banner inches in front of the cat. The crowd pulled Cindy along on their way to congratulate Ray.

"Thanks, Roscoe," he said, hugging him and letting the cat lick away the sweat on his face. "You're the only one who never gave up on me. As many times as I'd throw you out, you kept coming back."

"Meow." His bushy tail switched back and forth like a huge cattail caught in a storm.

"Don't worry. I won't ever give up again."

"I'm so proud of you, Ray." He turned and both he and Roscoe were smothered by Robin's large bosom as she wrapped them in a hearty embrace. "You know what this means, don't you?"

"Yeah. I can leave. But I'll visit. I know I'll be asking Roscoe for pointers when I start counseling. That's right," he said, seeing her surprise. "I figure I'd be good at dealing with people as messed up as I was when I came here."

"But you aren't anymore."

"Thanks to Roscoe." Making sure his friend was secure in his lap, he excused himself and wheeled over to the group waiting for him.

"What did he mean?" Cindy asked. "What did Roscoe do?"

"We're really not sure. Ray used to throw Roscoe off his bed whenever he'd visit. He even bounced him off the wall once. We'd shut the door to his room so Roscoe couldn't get in – we were afraid for him. But somehow he always managed to sneak in." Robin scratched her head and adjusted her cap. "I guess his persistence paid off because one day I went in to give Ray his lunch, and they were playing tag."

"Tag?"

"Well, their version. Roscoe would jump on his bed, smack him and then run down to the foot of it just out of his reach. Ray'd have to sit up and lean over to tag him back. They'd do this over and over. I wouldn't have believed it either if I hadn't seen it," she said when Cindy rolled her eyes.

33

"But playing that silly game built up Ray's strength and confidence. Pretty soon he was in the wheelchair chasing Roscoe around the room. From there they'd race up and down the halls. He improved so much that we told him the day he beats Roscoe is the day he can be released."

"It looks like his attitude changed, too."

Robin nodded. "As he got stronger, so did his belief in himself. Now he's Mr. Personality. All the old ladies love him."

"Hard to believe a cat could accomplish what we couldn't. Makes you feel kind of stupid, doesn't it?"

"Not stupid. More like ashamed."

Thinking back to Mrs. Shannon, Cindy's face reddened.

The rest of the day Cindy trailed behind the energetic ball of fur on his rounds. She left at the end of the day still wondering how this assignment was going to solve her problem. "Maybe I need to glue fake fur on myself and wear a collar," she muttered sarcastically on her drive home.

She knew animals were therapeutic for patients, but a nurse's job involved more than just lying on someone's lap. But yet, Roscoe seemed to do more than that. *But what?* She mulled it over during dinner and went to bed early, tossing and turning all night trying to figure it out.

The next day she drove to work arguing with herself. *Trust Kris a little longer. Isn't that what she'd asked of me? Then why do I want to see Roscoe fail?* She forced herself to admit it was because it hurt to be compared to a stray cat and come up lacking. Still stewing, she entered the nursing home to see Beth waiting for her.

"Sorry I didn't get a chance to check with you before you left yesterday. How's it going?"

Cindy paused. "Honestly?"

Beth nodded, encouraging her to continue.

"I don't see the point. What's a cat got to do with helping me get back whatever it was I lost? Nurses can't act like Roscoe."

"Is he really doing anything we can't do?" She lowered her head slightly and looked at Cindy over her bifocals. "Think about it." Without another word, she walked away.

This is nuts. How can I learn if no one tells me anything? Anger drove her towards the exit, but a mound of fur was standing guard at the door.

"You think you're going to stop me?" she yelled.

Roscoe cocked his head to one side, his emerald eyes staring back at her. Ashamed at her outburst, she knelt and ran her fingers through his thick fur. "I'm just so angry...no...confused. Nursing is all I ever wanted to do. But how can you possibly help me?"

"MmeeOOWWW!"

Startled, she fell backwards landing on her rear. A second later Roscoe was standing in her lap, licking the tears running down her face.

"I want to be a good nurse," she pleaded. "I just don't know how anymore." Like a child clinging to a security blanket, she wrapped her arms around him.

Calmed by his steady purring, she took a deep breath and sniffed back her tears before setting Roscoe on the floor in front of her. For several seconds his green eyes drew her in as the still elusive emotion she'd seen the first day played across them. "OK, my furry friend. I'm desperate. If Kris thinks you can help, I'll believe in you, too. No questions asked. Teach me. Please," she begged.

Sounding more like a bird when he answered her with a deep chirp, Roscoe headed down the hall. She quickly got to her feet and ran after him.

Throughout the day she shadowed him diligently. Many of their visits took less than ten minutes, but Cindy saw the appreciation in peoples' eyes at being remembered. Those too ill to do anything but lie in bed drew comfort from his warm body when he took catnaps with them. Others, their minds still intact, but trapped in bodies too disabled to function independently, had their spirits jump-started by Roscoe's special attention. She saw the results of his actions but still couldn't comprehend his secret.

However, when they entered Mrs. Barton's room, an Alzheimer's patient who'd been admitted the day before, Cindy doubted whether even Roscoe could work his magic. The room was in chaos. Broken dishes were scattered around the floor. Gravy and clumps of mashed potatoes dripped down one wall. The sheets had been ripped from the bed and dangled over the edge like a waterfall. The tray was upside down on the floor with a large piece missing from the corner.

Robin looked as if she was wrestling a steer as she struggled to keep the woman, her frantic gyrations bringing her close to the edge, from falling out of bed.

She rushed to her aid. "What's going on?"

"She suddenly went ballistic," Robin said. "Grab her other arm so she can't hit us. I need to give her a sedative."

Ducking her head when the woman swung at her, Cindy grabbed it, amazed at the frail woman's strength. "What set her off?"

"She started talking to me like I was her husband. When I told her he wasn't here, she refused to believe me, and went off." She wiped off the sweat dripping down her forehead.

"Has anyone called her husband?"

"He's dead. It's been several years, but her mind's so far gone, poor thing, she doesn't remember. She keeps calling to him. Henry, Henry," she said, mimicking the woman. "It's so pitiful."

"Henry. I knew you'd come." The woman, exhausted from her tirade, collapsed against the pillows. "Remember the pretty flowers in the garden, Henry? They brightened up the house so much. Go cut me some now. Please."

"See what I mean?" Robin said.

"Henry. Talk to me." The woman, her white hair damp from exertion, continued shouting his name. Cindy tightened her hold again as she felt the stirrings of another outburst.

"Where's Roscoe?" Cindy looked around and spotted him in the corner. "Roscoe, what are you doing over there? Get over here and help us."

But the cat remained glued where he was, his attention riveted on Mrs. Barton.

Once the sedative took effect, Cindy's anger at Roscoe's indifference flared up, and she turned to reprimand him, but only saw the end of his black tail as he ran through the doorway.

You did nothing, Roscoe. Why? I believed in you. How could you ignore that poor woman?

The next day she forgot her doubts when she saw the smiles on the faces of all he visited during the day. When they reached Mrs. Barton's room she was confident he'd redeem himself from yesterday's behavior.

Lying quietly in bed, she stirred when they entered. "Henry. It's so nice to see you."

Cindy quickly went to her side. "Hello, Mrs. Barton. It's me, Cindy."

"Henry, I missed you."

"No dear. I'm Cindy."

"Don't tease me," she shouted. "Where are the flowers you promised to bring me?"

"Just relax," Cindy said, smoothing the wispy curls from the lady's forehead.

"Don't touch me," she screamed, shoving Cindy backwards.

Thrown off balance, Cindy recovered quickly when the woman suddenly sat up and swung her legs over the side of the bed. Grabbing her with one hand, Cindy pushed the call button with the other and held on, hoping help would come before she lost her grip.

"Roscoe," she hissed. "Don't just sit there. Do something." Her irritation grew with every second that the cat sat calmly in the corner watching them struggle. "What's wrong with you," she shouted. "Get over – thank God you came," Cindy gasped when Robin ran into the room "I don't think I could've held her much longer."

While Robin gave the woman a shot and held her until it took effect, Cindy straightened the sheets and tucked them around her. As soon as she felt Robin could handle things alone, she whipped around to unleash her fury, but Roscoe was already dashing out the door.

"You're not getting away this time," she shouted, chasing after him. Focused only on her quarry, she plowed into a cart of lunch trays in the middle of the hall. By the time she'd cleaned up the mess, Roscoe was nowhere in sight.

Even after she left work and went home she was unable to forget Roscoe and fumed all evening. *What's gotten into that cat? How could he just sit and watch when he knew Mrs. Barton was so upset? Couldn't he tell the poor lady was hurting? Why, he's no better than I am.* Several times she picked up the phone to call Kris and ream her for wasting her time, only to slam the receiver down.

Too keyed up to sleep, she put on her running shoes and hurried from the apartment. Fueled by her anger and frustration, she ran an extra two miles until her sides were heaving and her mind was free of her toxic thoughts. Walking home, she convinced herself that there had to be a reason for Roscoe's unusual behavior.

Entering the nursing home the next morning, Cindy was filled with a mixture of anticipation and dread. Today was her last day. Her last chance to discover the answer she'd been sent here to find. *What if I don't find it?* Her pulse quickened in response, and she said a silent prayer that Roscoe wouldn't let her down again.

Beth, who'd arrived at the same time, fell into step beside her. "How's it going, Cindy?"

"I'm not sure. I've seen Roscoe do some wonderful things, but…"

"Go on," Beth prompted.

"Well…at first I was amazed at how he worked with the patients." Hesitating to voice her doubts, she paused. Suddenly her frustration of the last week flew out. "To be blunt, he's disappointed me the last couple of days."

"Oh?" Beth said, stopping next to the door of her first patient of the day. "What happened?"

"All he does is watch Mrs. Barton. Won't go near her. The poor woman's really having a rough time. He's ignoring her when she needs him the most."

"Ah. But she's a new patient, isn't she?"

"Yes. But what's that got to do with it?"

"A great deal. In fact, that's Roscoe's greatest gift."

"What?"

"It's important that you discover that for yourself." Dismissing her with a Cheshire grin, Beth pushed open the patient's door and went inside.

Why won't anyone give me any answers! Determined not to spoil her last day, she put her shoulders back and uttered a pleasant greeting to the patient she passed on her way down the hall.

The morning passed quickly, and Cindy was relieved to see that Roscoe was as charming as ever with the patients. She was aware of every nuance he made, intent on solving the riddle that still haunted her. But by lunchtime it still escaped her. It was like working on a jigsaw puzzle that had a missing piece.

On her afternoon break she decided to say goodbye to Mrs. Howell, the first patient she'd met that week. At first glance she thought she'd gone into the wrong room, not recognizing the woman, her face no longer ghostly pale, smiling back at her.

"You're looking well, Mrs. Howell."

"Thank you, dear. Yes. I've been eating like a good girl." She giggled.

"That's wonderful." Cindy took her outstretched hand. "I've come to say good-bye. Today's my last day here."

"Well, I'll be sorry to see you go. I've noticed Roscoe's been your constant companion."

"Yes. Believe it or not, I was here to learn from him."

Expecting her to laugh, Cindy was shocked when Mrs. Howell said, "You know, he's wiser than most humans I know. You'll be a better nurse for having known him."

"What do you mean?"

"It's really quite simple, my dear. Unfortunately, most people are too busy or caught up in their own lives to see it." Patting Cindy's hand, she said, "Now you have a pleasant day. Time for me to write a note to my grandson."

After handing her the stationary from the bedside table, Cindy continued down the hall, mulling over what she'd just been told. *What am I not seeing? Why can everyone else see it but I can't?* Noticing the time, she quickened her steps. Time to check on Mrs. Barton.

She found her sleeping peacefully. Not finding Roscoe in his usual place in the corner, she was hopeful that today he'd atone for his bewildering behavior. *He must be running a little late.* She sat down to wait for him, careful not to disturb the sleeping woman. She admitted she was a bit uncomfortable handling her alone.

But when half an hour passed with no sign of him, she reluctantly got up to wake her for her sponge bath. *Don't take your anger at him out on her,* she cautioned herself.

"Mrs. Barton," she said, gently touching her shoulder.

Her eyes snapped open. "Hello, Henry."

"No, I'm Cindy. Remember?"

"Who? I guess Henry's late today. I wish he'd get here," she cried, rocking back and forth, her feet beginning to jiggle.

Dreading another episode like yesterday, Cindy talked quietly to the woman, massaging her shoulders. But her efforts failed, and Mrs. Barton began whimpering and rocking from side to side, her agitation increasing with each movement. Just when she'd decided to push the button for help, Roscoe brushed her arm aside when he jumped onto the bed.

"I knew you'd come, Henry." Mrs. Barton suddenly grew still, her face bright with anticipation.

"Meow." A small bouquet of flowers dropped from his mouth.

"Oh, you remembered, darling." Picking it up, she sunk her nose into its center and breathed deeply. "They're beautiful. My favorites." She patted the covers next to her and smiled at him when he sat down, leaning his body against her hip.

"Tell me about your day."

"Puuuuuuuurrrrrrrrrrrrr. Ccchhiirrrrrrp. MMMMeeeoowwww."

Listening to the unorthodox conversation, Cindy saw Mrs. Barton turn into a sweet and witty lady as she responded to Roscoe's chatter.

What had he done to cause this transformation? But no answer came. Her ineptness hit her like a torpedo. *I don't deserve to wear this uniform.*

Her thoughts were interrupted when Roscoe kissed Mrs. Baron's nose and jumped off the bed to leave. Cindy dragged her feet, heavy as sandbags, down the hall behind him. Reaching the reception counter, Roscoe vaulted onto it and waited for her to catch up. She slumped against it and began petting the cat she'd grown to love.

"It's no use, Roscoe. I can't find it." She gulped back the sobs percolating in her belly.

"Yeeeoowwwwwwwwl." His mournful wail matched the sorrow in his eyes.

She knew he was trying to communicate with her. "It's no use. I was stupid to think I should ever be a nurse." She hugged him tightly. "It's not your fault," she said and ran from the building, stumbling through her fog of tears.

Dusk was just beginning to settle when Cindy woke up. She'd cried all the way home, and after throwing herself on her bed, a new dam of tears had broken loose until, exhausted, she'd fallen asleep. Sitting up, she rubbed her puffy and bloodshot eyes and reached for a tissue. After blowing her nose, which was as red as her eyes, she tossed it next to the wastebasket already overflowing with them.

"I just don't have what it takes." Like a thief who's just heard a guilty verdict delivered by a jury, she could no longer deny the truth. "At least I tried. But now I know." *Kris will be so disappointed in me.*

She wandered lethargically through the apartment, but finally decided she had to do something constructive, however slight. *I won't need these anymore,* she thought, gathering up her uniforms to drop off at Briarwood. *I'm sure someone can use them.* Thinking back to her last day there she realized there was something else she needed to do when she got there.

Walking into Briarwood a short time later, Cindy was relieved to see no one in the lobby and left the box of uniforms on the desk. She hurried down the hall to Mrs. Shannon's room hoping she wouldn't run into any of her coworkers. She flinched at the thought of having to tell them she'd no longer be working here, or anywhere, as a nurse.

Quietly opening the door, she peeked in and saw the woman reading. She closed the door behind her and walked halfway into the room.

"Hello, Mrs. Shannon."

Fear flickered in the woman's eyes as recognition dawned.

"Please. May I talk to you?" Before she could be told to leave, she hurried on. "I want to apologize. I was so mean to you. For no reason. It was all my fault." She lowered her head in shame before looking at her again. "You didn't deserve to be treated like that. And I'm sincerely sorry."

The woman held out her hand, and Cindy noticed for the first time the gnarled and twisted fingers with knuckles that looked like giant stones. "Why don't you come closer and bring that chair so you can sit down."

The following Monday when Kris went to her office, the first thing she did was to go over to the red folder. She opened it, confident she'd find it empty. Instead, Cindy's letter jumped out at her. She dropped into her chair. "I don't believe it," she said, dropping her head into hands. "It's impossible." She reached for the small framed photo at the edge of her desk. "Roscoe, what happened? Of all the nurses I've sent to you, Cindy was the one I never had any doubts about."

She reached for the phone to call Beth but dropped it back into its cradle. "I better think this through first." Leaving her office, she walked with her head down, absorbed with her thoughts. As she passed Mrs. Shannon's room she heard a strange tapping and went in to investigate.

"Cindy," she cried.

"Hi, Kris."

"What are you doing here?"

"What do you mean?" Her confusion was evident.

"But your letter. It's—"

"Oh. The letter." She hit her head with the heel of her hand. "I was so excited to start our project that I forgot all about it." She waved her hand in the air. "Tear it up." Grinning broadly, she leaned over the bed and touched Mrs. Shannon's hand. "Would you excuse me for just a minute."

"Of course, dear."

She hurried over to Kris. "When I left Roscoe on Friday I'd given up any thoughts of nursing. I still hadn't found the answer. I was devastated, but I knew it was the right thing to do."

Kris started to speak, but Cindy put out her hand to stop her. "Then I came here to apologize to Mrs. Shannon and everything clicked." Like a pirate who's discovered a buried treasure, her eyes sparkled with excitement, and she impulsively hugged her supervisor.

"Mrs. Shannon and I had such a lovely visit. We talked for hours. The time flew by." She smiled back at Mrs. Shannon and left Kris to return to her chair by the bed. "She's had quite life, haven't you?" She squeezed the woman's forearm gently and looked over at Kris. "Did you know she used to be an English teacher? But her big dream was to write a novel. Unfortunately, that became impossible when her arthritis became so debilitating. So…"

Cindy and Mrs. Shannon looked at each other like two children hiding a secret and then burst into laughter. "So," Cindy repeated, "during my lunch hours and on Saturday mornings before my shift starts, I'm going to be her hands." She held up her laptop like she'd won a prize.

Her eyes bright with unshed tears, Kris said, "That's wonderful. "I'll leave you two to get back to your fun." Before closing the door, she said, "I want the first autographed copy."

Returning to her office, Kris picked up Cindy's letter and ripped it in half before tossing it into the trash. She picked up Roscoe's picture and stared into the large emerald eyes that seemed to wink back at her. "Thanks, Roscoe. You saved another one."

Unconditional Love

The seeds for this book were planted almost thirty-five years ago on the day my first cat died. My guilt at not being with her at that time has haunted me since. To never have been able to say, "I love you" one more time, or to comfort her as she'd comforted me so many times, still causes my heart to ache.

By writing the following story, I think I've finally exorcised those demons. This story is for you, Faygo. Thank you, dear friend, for starting me on my life-long journey as a cat lover and for teaching me the true meaning of unconditional love.

Oh, one more thing: "I love you."

A cold, unforgiving silence greeted Sara when she entered the house. She hurried to Molly's bed to check on her. Empty. Even the small afghan she'd crocheted was gone. She ran through the house searching for her.

"Molly? Where are you? Please just be hiding," she prayed. Intent on her mission, Sara almost ran into her mother who was standing with her arms crossed at the end of the hall, her nostrils flaring.

"You're too late," her mother snarled. "Molly died an hour ago. I'm sure she hates you for not being there for her."

The words slammed into her as if a barrage of bullets had attacked her. She slumped against the wall.

"Hope your precious party was worth it."

Her mother's last dig caused a fresh stream of tears to spill down her face.

Sara turned and raced back down the hall trying to escape the mounting guilt closing in on her. Tripping over the rug in the utility room, she pushed herself up off the floor, never losing momentum, and rushed outside. She jumped into her car and peeled out of the driveway oblivious to the curses from the owner of a black Sable she narrowly missed.

"I'm so sorry." She repeated the words over and over like a mantra. Instead of peace, however, anguish tore through her gut. The vet had explained that Molly's kidneys were shutting down, but Sara had never expected her to go so soon.

She drove aimlessly through the darkness, her vision blurred by the constant stream of tears. The car's interior echoed with her sobs. At a four-way stop she rifled through her purse and pulled out a photo from the roll she'd picked up that morning. Her eyes bore into the image.

"Oh, Molly. I'm so sorry. Can you forgive me?" she cried. Dropping her head, she whispered, "Can I forgive myself?"

Mother was right. I'm a bad person. I never thought I was. I'm on the honor roll. Don't smoke, drink, or take drugs. Barely been kissed, let alone slept with anyone. But Mom's right. I am bad. If only I hadn't gone to Laura's party.

But Rick was going, the first boy to show any interest in being more than just friends. The guilt at her selfishness spread through her body like a metastasized cancer. "Molly, you're right to hate me."

The blast of a horn jerked her to attention, and she floored the gas pedal, putting space between her and the car behind her. She drove with no direction in mind, engulfed in her tortured thoughts.

Three hours later, lost and tired, she pulled into a deserted parking lot and parked beneath a light pole. She ran her fingers through her disheveled blonde hair and looked again at the photo clutched in her hand, gently running her fingertips over the image. The finality of her friend's death sliced through her like a saber. Sobs tore through her body, and she struck the steering wheel over and over again. "And now you're gone…And you'll never know how much I loved you…How I never meant to hurt you…How much comfort you gave me."

She sagged against the seat. "Oh, Molly. I'm sorry. Oh God, please let her hear me," she pleaded. Flashbacks of their friendship whirled through her mind. Looking at her picture again, her thoughts latched onto the one, thirteen years ago, when they'd first met.

"Yeowwwlll!"

Sara stopped building her castle in the sandbox and looked over at the rosebushes. She squealed in delight when a tiny kitten stuck its head out from beneath one and wobbled over to her.

"Mommy, look what I found." She picked up the scraggly kitten under its arms, leaving its body to dangle, flopping back and forth as she ran over to her mother who was hanging freshly laundered clothes on the line to dry. "Can I keep it, Mommy?" Sara begged.

"No. You're too young," her mother said, taking a clothespin out of her mouth.

"I'm four years old, the same age as Patty, and she's got a kitty."

"Well, Patty isn't as unreliable as you are. I'd only end up taking care of it." Her mother turned her back and began hanging a shirt on the clothesline.

Determined to prove her wrong, Sara carried it into the house and went into the kitchen. After pouring milk into a bowl, she sat on the floor giggling at the pink tongue darting in and out as the kitten devoured the milk. Once the bowl was licked clean, the kitten looked up at her and began purring.

"You're thanking me." Sara clapped her hands gleefully.

"What do you think you're doing?"

Sara's joy dissolved when she saw her mother in the doorway, a scowl on her face. "I wanted to show you I can take care of it."

The tiny creature walked unsteadily over to her. Extending its razor-sharp claws, it pulled itself onto her lap, turned around once, plopped down, and immediately went to sleep.

Sara grinned up at her mother. "See. It knows it belongs with me."

With her hands on her hips, her mother shouted, "I told you—"

"Grace? Sara? Where is everybody?"

"Daddy," Sara shouted. "Come look what I found."

"Well, what have we here?" her father asked when he walked into the kitchen, almost stepping on the ball of fur that had awoken at Sara's shouts and was now exploring the room.

Running into her father's arms and squirming with excitement, Sara looked up at him, her eyes squinting as she pleaded, "Can I keep it? Huh, Daddy? Please."

"Walt, tell her she can't—"

"How can I say no to my best girl?" He ignored the incensed look on Grace's face.

"Oh thank you, Daddy." She started over to the kitten, but ran back to her father and gave him a hug before returning to her new friend. Sitting down in front of it, she traced the brown markings that ran like ribbons from head to tail through the buttermilk undercoat. "Isn't it beautiful?" Sara said breathlessly. The kitten, as if it knew it was being inspected, turned over and stuck its tiny white paws in the air.

"It sure is, darling. What are you going to call it?"

Frowning in concentration, Sara said, "Well, I always wanted a sister named Molly."

"Then Molly it'll be," her father said. Keenly aware of the smoldering anger in his wife's eyes, he turned serious. "This is a big responsibility. You can handle it though, can't you?"

"Oh yes, Daddy." Sara pointed proudly to the empty bowl. "I already fed her."

Grace's snort filled the air. "Yeah, just look at the mess you made. Milk all over the floor."

Walt shot his wife a look of disgust. "Don't worry. Sara and I'll clean it up."

"Darn right you will," Grace said before stomping out of the room.

Tears formed at the corners of Sara's eyes. Walt quickly leaned over and gave her a kiss. "Don't worry about her. She'll come around. She's just tired."

Sara stared at Molly's picture wishing her friend could hear her. "She finally did accept you. But not me. No, never me," she said wistfully. "At least I had you, Molly. You were the best playmate. So patient. Remember those old doll clothes I'd dress you up in? You'd lie there in that doll buggy with your paws sticking out of those silly dresses, never crying or trying to get away. How did you put up with all the stupid things I did to you?" Her face pinched with grief as she remembered an even crueler incident when she was seven.

"What are you doing?" her mother screamed when she walked into the living room.

"I'm making Molly fly. Like Sylvester in the cartoon," Sara said, twirling the cat in a circle by her ears.

"You idiot! That's make-believe. You're hurting her." She grabbed Molly out of Sara's hands and gently rubbed the cat's ears before putting her down. Standing up, she reached over and yanked hard on Sara's ear, ignoring the young child's cries. "I bet Molly won't ever play with you again, and it would serve you right."

Still thinking of the cruel but unintentional pain she'd caused her cat, Sara adjusted the seat of the car to give her legs more room. "But Mom was wrong, wasn't she, Molly? I'm the one that ran and hid under my bed – I was so ashamed – and you're the one who came and laid down next to me and licked my tears away as if you were saying, 'It's all right. I know you didn't mean it.'"

She arched her back to relieve a persistent kink before leaning back again. "But Mom never let me forget that or all the hundred other times she thought I'd done something wrong."

Like dominos, other memories of her mother's sharp tongue exploded to the surface, one on top of another: "If you were more athletic you'd have gotten first place instead of second. I bet you're the only girl in the class who doesn't have a date to the prom. No boy's ever going to look at you if you don't lose some weight. We aren't paying tuition to a private school just so you can get Bs."

"Why can't I ever please her?" Her fist pounded the console in time to her words. "Why? Why? Why?" She gasped for air in between her sobs and frantically searched for Molly's picture. Spotting it on the floor, she grabbed it, clutching it to her chest, as if by holding it close she'd be able to feel Molly's soothing presence.

Slowly her breathing returned to normal, and her eyes returned to the picture. "You never judged me, did you, girl? You just accepted me the way

I was. Why can't Mom understand me like you did?"

Shaking her head sadly, she tucked a loose strand of hair behind her ear. She wished her father's job didn't take him away from home for days at a time. His phone calls, even with their encouraging words, failed to take away the sting of her mother's constant criticism. Molly'd been her steady source of support. *Who'll act as my buffer now?*

Loneliness descended upon her like a shroud. Panic bubbled up from her belly, and she began shaking despite the warm night air. Fighting to gain control, she closed her eyes and focused on the pleasant times with Molly. Slowly her anxiety lessened, and she let the exhaustion take over. Her final thoughts as she fell asleep were of the time, a year ago, when Molly had provided the comfort that had been so lacking from her mother.

"Mom, I feel terrible," Sara said, shivering despite the warmth of the down-filled comforter.

"What do you expect?" Grace said. "You've got a bad case of strep throat. It's infected your vocal chords."

"What does that mean? That I'll lose my voice forever?" Sara looked anxiously at her mother for reassurance.

"It'd serve you right if you did. How stupid can you get for going sledding without a hat or long underwear on? You were soaked clear through."

"I didn't think it would be that cold."

"That's right. You didn't think. As usual," her mother said, opening the bottle of antibiotics the doctor had prescribed. "Here. Take these." Her foot tapped impatiently while Sara slowly sat up. She ignored the grimace on her daughter's face as she swallowed the pills.

Before Sara could lie back down, her mother walked to the door to leave. "Mom, can't you stay awhile?"

"I've got work to do. Even more now that you can't help."

"But it feels like I'm choking every time I swallow. It's scary."

"Stop being such a baby."

Her mother's disgust was evident to Sara, and she fought back her tears knowing they'd only give her mother another reason to criticize her. "I'm sorry."

"Well, sorry isn't going to get the house clean," Grace said, slamming the door behind her.

The tears Sara had held in came crashing out, and she pulled the covers over her head to muffle them.

"Meow."

She uncovered the covers in time to see Molly get up from the foot of the bed and walk over to her. The cat delicately stepped onto Sara's chest and lowered herself, before gingerly crawling forward until her whiskers brushed Sara's chin.

"Oh, Molly," she moaned. "I feel like I'm buried in ice, and a firecracker's exploded in my throat."

Wrapping her paws around the girl's neck, Molly flattened her body across Sara's as if she were trying to absorb her pain and raging fever. Her steady purring slowly lulled Sara to sleep.

The warmth of her surroundings woke Sara. Still half asleep, she rolled the car window down, and as she fell asleep, another dream surfaced.

Getting into her car, she headed to Patty's. Five miles down the road she banked for a curve and felt the car's rear end slide on the wet pavement. Overreacting, she jerked the steering wheel and slammed on the brakes, sending the car into a skid and directly towards a row of trees lining the road. Screaming, she threw her hands up to cover her face and waited for the impact.

Her body snapped forward when the car came to a sudden stop. She looked out the window and saw that the back bumper was caught on a dead tree limb. Seconds later the car began to teeter, and she watched in horror as the limb snapped. She was slammed against the seat when the car plummeted straight down, landing with a muffled plop in the ditch. Looking out the window, she saw thick, slimy mud, the consistency of unbaked brownie dough, rising steadily around the car.

"Help." Only the burping of the quicksand answered her screams. "Nooooo. Molly. Help me, Molly."

Sara's frantic screams jolted her awake. Her heart pounded and her sweat-drenched body caused her to shiver. Instead of being relieved that it was only a nightmare, tears ran down her cheeks.

It's funny how you're the one I called to for help, she thought. *But you always put me first. Like that time I was so sick. You never left my side except to use the litter box. You would've starved if Dad hadn't brought your food to you.* She clutched her body with her arms and moaned as her selfishness hammered into her. *I never even thanked you for staying with me. Or for all the other times you gave me the love I craved.* Guilt consumed her. Like quicksand.

Startled by the slamming of car doors, she noticed people entering a church that abutted the lot. As if directed by a hypnotic suggestion, Sara followed them inside and settled into a back pew.

A minister walked down the center aisle to the podium. When he faced the congregation, his hazel eyes were warm with kindness. "I want to start my sermon today with a question. Who was the first person to give you unconditional love?"

Shutting her eyes, Sara silently answered his question. A smile broke across her face. Unobtrusively, she stood and walked from the church.

Three hours later Sara pulled into her driveway. Her father came running out of the house.

"Are you all right? I was worried sick," he said.

"I'm fine," she said, getting out of the car with a bouquet of daisies in her hand. "Sorry I didn't call."

"The important thing is you're all right," her father said, hugging her. "Listen, honey, your mother didn't mean to be so hard on you."

Pulling back from his embrace, Sara said, "Yes, she did. I know I'll never please her. I don't know why, but I probably never will."

"It's nothing you've done. She's –"

She shook her head. "It's OK, Dad. I know it's not my fault. She's the one with the problem. I'm not a bad person. And she's wrong about Molly hating me, too." She looked around for a moment before asking, "Where is she?"

"She's in her favorite spot."

Sara kissed him. "I'll be in shortly."

"Take your time, honey." He watched her until she went around the corner of the house.

51

When Sara entered the backyard she went immediately over to the flower garden. Usually bright with color from the variety of flowers planted there, it looked pale and somber now. Only the Russian Sage and dahlias swayed in the breeze. Gone were the phlox, day lilies, geraniums, and snapdragons. In their place was a circle of bare earth, its center slightly raised. Sara smiled slightly when she noticed that her father had left Molly's favorite flowers, the daisies, undisturbed. They formed a rim around her grave.

She kneeled down and put her hand on the raised spot. "You always looked so content when you took your afternoon nap here. You sure did love the warmth from the sun." She looked up and saw a blanket of ominous gray clouds. *It's fitting that there's no sun today.*

A single tear slowly ran down her cheek and fell onto the bare soil. Sara watched it sink into the ground. "I'm so sorry I wasn't with you. To hold you one last time. To let you know how much you meant to me."

Leaning over, she carefully spread the fresh daisies over the grave making sure that the spot where Molly lay was covered. "I already miss the feel of your wet nose on mine." She paused to swallow back a sob. "Oh, Molly, I loved you so much. But you already knew that, didn't you? Who'd ever think a cat would be wiser than people about love?" Picking up one of the daisies, she kissed its center and placed it back on the grave.

"Mom could take lessons from you. I know she won't change. And I'm not sure I'll be able to handle her rejections without you." She shuddered at the thought. For several minutes she stared into the daisies that formed a bright canopy over her friend. Then a light replaced the sadness in her eyes. "I know, Molly. I'll just pretend you're next to me, helping me through the bad times. OK?"

A ray of sunshine broke through the storm clouds and embraced the spot where Sara knelt. She raised her head and felt its warmth. "Sleep well, my friend."

A Nosy Solution

"Great dinner, Hon," Jake said, pushing his empty plate aside to make room for dessert.

"I thought we deserved an extra special one after all the work we did today." Rachel smiled as she set a piece of strawberry pie in front of him. "I never realized all the stuff we'd accumulated. We should've had a garage sale before we moved."

"That would've been hard to do on such short notice." Her husband looked at their daughter who'd remained silent through most of the meal. "How about you, Carly? What do you think of your new house?"

"My room is awesome," she said, her eyes dancing. Like a dam exploding, her sentences ran together in a flood of words. "I already met Franny, the girl next door. We're both in the same grade, and she told me we can walk to school together, and she'll show me around. She says our teacher's real nice."

She took a quick breath. "I'm going to miss Suzy and my friends from back home, but I'll make new ones here. So," she said, gulping down her last forkful, "I'll actually have more friends." She pushed herself away from the table and started to get up. "Can I be excused? Fran said we can go swimming. They've got a gigantic pool."

"I guess so, sweetie." Her father laughed at his daughter's verbal diarrhea. "You were a big help today." Before he could say another word, she was halfway across the room. "But don't you want dessert?"

"Later."

Jake looked at Rachel and rolled his eyes after the door slammed. "And to think I was so concerned about how she'd handle this. It's an awful big change for her. Leaving all her friends in California to come to Ohio."

"She's always been the adaptable one in the family. By the time school starts she'll probably know all the kids in her class." She took the last bite of pie. "Everything's working out. The house is great, the neighbors seem nice, and I'm so proud of you." She reached across the table and squeezed his hand. "Manager of Special Projects. Sounds mighty impressive."

Jake's smile turned into a frown. "You know I'll be working some long hours for awhile 'til I get a handle on my new responsibilities."

"This was a family decision, remember? We knew when you took the promotion it meant a transfer and some long hours up front. Besides," she said, starting to clear the table, "I'm looking forward to exploring your home town and seeing the places you've talked about." She walked into the kitchen. "I only wish your father knew you were back so he could see how well you've done."

Anger and sorrow swept across Jake's face. He stood up and threw his napkin next to his plate.

Hastily piling the dirty dishes on the counter, Rachel retraced her steps and stopped Jake before he left the room. She took his hand and waited for him to look at her. "I'm sorry, dear. That was thoughtless of me. I didn't mean to ruin the day."

He ran his hand through his hair and gave her a half smile. "I know. I thought I was over that. I didn't realize it could still get to me after all these years. It still hurts, though." He shrugged. "But he made the decision to wipe us from his life. Heck, he doesn't even know he has a granddaughter." He forced himself not to dwell on the painful subject. "Let's leave the dishes and take a walk. We can go to the park and sit by the river."

"And you can tell me some of the spots Carly and I should check out."

Four blocks to their north, Whitey, a sixty-year old widower, was going through his evening ritual. Tiptoeing out to the utility room, he lifted the container of food and gave it a quick shake. A moment later he heard the pounding of feet running down the hall.

A cat, its long coat as white as a freshly bleached bed sheet except for what looked like splotches of dirt in the middle of its forehead and on its paws, galloped into the room.

"I think you broke your record, Nosy." He held her food bowl just out of reach. The short, high-pitched meows told him he'd teased her enough. Setting the dish down, Nosy ignored the pat on her rump and stuck her head into the bowl. While she was eating he refilled the other dish with fresh water.

"Now it's my turn." He warmed up the leftovers from the night before and ate while scanning a magazine. When he was done he quickly washed the few dishes and went into the living room to sit down. Pulling the handle of the footrest, he moved his legs to one side. Nosy jumped up a second later to join him, stretching her body to its full length beside him. Within moments she was asleep. He absently petted her while he channel surfed, finally deciding on a rerun of his favorite murder mystery.

Halfway through it he lifted himself from the chair, careful not to disturb the snoozing cat, and went out to the kitchen to make popcorn. When he returned Nosy was sitting up wide-awake, her eyes, as big as marbles, fixated on the bowl in his hand. He took his time eating it, one kernel at a time, stealing glances at the cat who followed each kernel on its path to his mouth. Every so often, like a boxer, she'd throw a quick jab with her paw, knocking one from his fingers. "You're the only cat I know that likes popcorn." He chuckled as she retrieved it with her tongue.

Deciding not to watch the eleven o'clock news, Whitey turned off the TV and checked to make sure the doors were locked. Returning to the utility room, he scooped out a handful of treats and walked down the hall to his bedroom, dropping them on the bed on his way to the bathroom. "You're quite the beggar, aren't you?" he said, listening to the sounds of a weak dustbuster as she inhaled them.

Finished in the bathroom, he got into bed and turned off the light. He felt Nosy kneading the covers before dropping down next to him like a sack of sand. Enveloping her curled body in the crook of his arm, they quickly fell asleep.

The next morning Whitey decided to take advantage of the sunny day and was trimming the hedges when the mail truck pulled up in front. He turned off the electric clippers and waved. "Hi, Steve. Where've you been?"

"On vacation. I went charter fishing in Florida with my brother," he said, walking over and handing him the mail.

"Catch anything?"

"You wouldn't believe it."

While they compared fish stories, Nosy, bored from sunning herself on the porch, strolled over to inspect the truck. She hopped through the opening and worked her way to the back, stopping to sniff the packages and stacks of mail. Finding a loose pile scattered in a large heap in the back, she nestled in the middle of it to take a nap.

She was jostled awake when the truck hit a large pothole. Standing up, she was knocked off her feet by the bouncing of the uneven pavement. Since Whitey's was his last stop, Nosy wasn't able to escape the roller coaster ride until Steve returned the truck to the post office. Curious with the new sights and smells, she set off to explore.

Several hours later, hungry and thirsty, Nosy crawled through some hedges into a backyard and spotted a trio of sparrows splashing in a birdbath. Slinking through the grass to within a few feet of her prey, she suddenly launched herself through the air. Instead of catching dinner, however, she landed with a plunk in the middle of the birdbath.

Standing up and shaking herself, she took advantage of the situation and lapped greedily, unaware of the overweight and irate woman waddling over with a broom in her hand. Her shrieks alerted Nosy, and she leaped from her perch just in time to avoid being swatted off. The cat sprinted from the yard, not slowing down until she'd covered two blocks and missed becoming fresh road kill by inches when she'd darted across the street in front of a car. Frightened and tired, the drenched cat crept beneath a cluster of bushes and quietly meowed.

As nightfall approached Whitey's irritation at Nosy's tardiness turned to worry. *It's not like her to miss her dinner.* Pacing from the porch to the kitchen and back again, his anxiety increased with each step. Needing to release some of his bottled up tension, he grabbed his windbreaker on the way out the door to look for her.

Two hours later, after covering all her favorite hangouts and failing to find her, he returned home, physically tired and emotionally drained. Knowing it was useless to even try to sleep, he sat in the dark and listened for her meow, much like a father who's anxiously waiting for his teenage son who's missed his curfew.

Towards dawn, stiff from sitting in the hard kitchen chair, Whitey moved to his easy chair. He raised the footrest and automatically moved his legs to the side, only to remember there was no need. He covered his face to try to control the tears from falling, and his body shook as he faced the fact that she'd become much more than just an animal to him. She was a friend who'd come into his life and showed him love when he'd needed it the most.

His thoughts traveled back to that painful time, twelve years ago, when his family dreams had been shattered. Reeling from his loss, he'd attempted to erase all reminders of that period by moving from his old neighborhood and ostracizing himself from his new neighbors. A bitter, lonely man replaced the once gregarious owner of the neighborhood restaurant. Resentment had been his only companion until the day he'd returned from his weekly trip for groceries and found a stray kitten sleeping in his porch swing.

Roughly pushing it off, he'd been surprised to find it curled between the sections of the paper the next morning. For three days he'd chased it away, but each morning it had greeted him with a meow from its post on the paper. On the fourth morning, when he'd kicked it, instead of running, it had looked at him for a moment before letting out a pitiful wail.

"You're as stubborn as I am." Never giving it a second glance before, he'd noticed the outline of its ribs poking out under the thinning and drab fur. "I guess I could give you some milk. Then you gotta git. I don't need no animal interfering in my life."

But when he'd gotten a quiet meow and a quick lick on his hand in thanks, the unapproachable armor he'd covered himself with began to crack. She'd gradually infiltrated that dark hole in his heart, and before he knew what was happening, she had the run of the house.

Whitey's kindhearted nature, kept so carefully hidden beneath a gruff exterior and earning him the reputation of "crotchety old coot," had blossomed. When he took his daily walks, now with Nosy beside him, people would come out to talk instead of running to avoid him.

The sound of the paperboy broke off his thoughts, and the full impact of Nosy's disappearance hit him. Always so in control, he started hyperventilating as a wave of helplessness washed over him. It took several deep breaths before his heart stopped racing. Thinking it would help if he kept busy, he got up and went to the kitchen to fix breakfast. Halfway through scrambling some eggs he noticed the time and ran to the phone to call the Humane Society to ask if anyone had dropped off a cat fitting Nosy's description.

"No, sir, I'm sorry. I suggest hanging posters for several blocks in all directions of your house with her picture and your address and phone number on it."

Ignoring his growling stomach, he turned the burner off, grabbed his favorite picture of Nosy, and went to the local copier store. Thirty minutes later, armed with three boxes of posters, he canvassed a square mile area, stopping strangers on the street and dropping posters off at every convenience store, grocery market, and gas station he passed.

The remaining posters he nailed to trees and telephone poles on his way home. His pace quickened the closer he got despite the blisters on his feet, and he clung to the hope she'd be resting in her favorite spot. As he turned into his front walk his shoulders slumped when he saw the empty porch swing.

The days dragged by with no response to the posters or the ad in the paper. His neighbors' well-meaning suggestions to replace her with another cat were met with icy glares. He refused to accept the growing possibility she wouldn't return. He began to withdraw, leaving the house only to run to the store for a few items, and echoes of past years reappeared.

The nights he was finally able to fall asleep were interrupted by nightmares. Visions of Nosy lying hurt, her head inches away from the drooling fangs of a Rotweiller, haunted him. On the tenth night of her disappearance Whitey tossed fitfully for hours before a restless sleep came just before dawn. Once again, he saw Nosy, her body covered in angry clusters of tangled fur around uneven patches of bare skin, desperately trying to crawl away from the snarling dog. Its snapping teeth, sounding like a staccato of hail on a metal roof, punctuated the air.

Whitey tried to run to her, but his legs refused to move. He reached down to fight off the unknown source that held him captive, but the more he struggled, the harder his opponent held him. Unable to save his beloved pet, he screamed to her to run and tried to inch himself closer by rolling along the ground.

Suddenly his body dropped into space, and he woke up to find himself on the floor wrapped like a mummy in his sheets. Whitey, his patience at an end, let out a bellow of rage. Thrashing his arms and legs to loosen the sheets, his foot punctured a hole through a worn spot. He grabbed the sheet at the tear and ripped it apart.

Drained at last, he fell forward, dropping his face into his open palms. His shoulders shook as he fought to gain his composure. Slowly he sat up and, shaking his head to clear the last vivid remnants of the nightmare away, he bent over to retrieve the threadbare and grass stained jeans and work shirt from the floor where he'd dropped them the night before.

He walked into the bathroom and glanced into the mirror above the sink. A stranger that could've passed for one of the derelicts living beneath the overpass south of town stared back at him. The ten-day old stubble on his face, and the unruly, thick hair sticking out haphazardly like torn cotton candy just enhanced his tormented image. Too tired to brush his teeth, he took a swig of mouthwash and swished it around before spitting it out.

Hungry despite the churning of his stomach, he headed down the hall, stopping when he heard the doorbell. After the third persistent ring, he cursed under his breath and stormed to the door. He yanked it open, primed to release his frustration on the unsuspecting caller, but his hostility died at the sight before him.

"Nosy," he shouted, grabbing the cat from the stranger's arms and hugging her tightly against his chest. "I thought I'd never see you again."

"I was hoping she was yours. She sure is glad to see you, Mister. She was sleeping under one of the park benches. I thought she looked like the picture in the poster. She's much skinnier now, though. And dirtier."

"Yes, she sure is, isn't she?" he said, holding the squalling cat at arm's length to inspect her. Her skin hung loosely on her like it was two sizes too big, and her once full coat of fur was matted with burrs. Finding nothing that a good bath, brushing, and food couldn't fix, he turned his attention to Nosy's savior. He guessed her to be about eight. Her mop of unruly red curls accented her green eyes, and she had a pair of dime-sized dimples in her cheeks.

"You're not from around here, are you?" he asked.

"No. I live about two miles that way," she said, pointing over her shoulder. "We just moved here. My name's Carly."

"Hello, Carly." He smiled when she formally extended her hand for him to shake. "My friends call my Whitey. Because of my hair. It turned snow-white ten years ago." He tried without success to smooth it down, embarrassed at his disheveled appearance.

"I can't thank you enough for returning her," he said, burying his face in Nosy's fur as if he needed to feel her to believe she was real. "Would you like to come in for a minute? I want to give you a reward."

"Oh, I don't want anything. I know how sad I'd be if I had a pet and it got lost."

"Well, I'd like to do something." He thought a moment. "I think I've got some cookies."

"That'd be great."

As soon as they stepped inside Nosy leapt from Whitey's arms and trotted to the back room.

"I see she hasn't forgotten where her food is." He laughed. "Would you like to feed her?"

She nodded vigorously.

"Go through the kitchen," he said, pointing. "The utility room's off it. The food's in the container on top of the washer. I'll get the cookies." While Carly was filling Nosy's bowl, Whitey rummaged through the cupboards. "I'm afraid all I've got are Oreo's, and they're probably stale."

"That's OK. Oreo's are my favorite."

When she came into the kitchen he pulled out a chair for her and placed a plate of cookies and a glass of milk in front of her. Taking one, she pulled it apart and licked off the white innards before popping the brown wafers in her mouth.

"That's how I eat them, too."

They both stopped talking while they munched. When Whitey reached for another cookie it was knocked out of his hand when Nosy jumped into his lap. All thoughts of the cookie were forgotten. Supporting her rump with one hand, he patted her back gently until she was lying comfortably against his chest, her head tucked under his chin.

"Do you live alone?" she asked.

He nodded. "Except for Nosy."

Carly's face softened at the odd picture before her. The man, built like a lumberjack, looked more suited to have a bull mastiff for a pet instead of the scrawny cat sleeping peacefully with its paws wrapped around his neck. His hand, large enough to crush a can with a quick squeeze, tenderly caressed the emaciated body.

When he glanced up she asked, "You're not married?"

He shook his head. "My wife died fifteen years ago."

"I'm sorry. Do you have any children?"

A spark of anger flickered in his eyes. "Not anymore," he said gruffly. "My son left years ago."

"You mean he died, too?"

"You could say that."

"Then I'm doubly glad I found her." She reached over and touched her nose. "Nosy. That's a funny name. How'd you pick that?"

"She used to poke her nose into everything as a kitten." He stroked the cat's head when she raised it at the sound of her name. "Looks like it got her into trouble this time."

Not used to the company of children, Whitey was quickly charmed by Carly's unabashed enthusiasm and quick wit, and he lost all track of time until the rumbling of his stomach broke into their conversation. He glanced at his watch. "I can't believe it's noon already. I can whip up something to eat if you'd like to stay for lunch."

"Gosh," she said, jumping up. "I gotta run. I forgot that Mom and Dad are taking me to lunch and the movies."

"Let me drive you home. It'll be faster."

Fifteen minutes later Carly directed him to pull into the driveway of a sprawling brick ranch situated at the end of a cul-de-sac in one of the new executive subdivisions. A slender but athletic woman in her early thirties looked up from the book she was reading and walked down the sidewalk towards them. Her face broke into the same infectious smile as Carly's.

"Mom, I found a lost cat," Carly shouted, running over to her. "And I returned her to her owner. This is Whitey. I wish you could've seen how happy Nosy was to be home. Isn't that a funny name, but it fits her. We had – "

"Hello, Whitey. I'm Rachel, Carly's mom. I hope she didn't talk your ear off." She laughed, putting her arm around her daughter's shoulders.

"Not at all. I enjoyed her company. I hope you didn't worry. I'm afraid we lost track of time. Have I made you late for the show?"

"No. We can always go to the later one." She turned to Carly. "But your dad's probably wondering what happened to us. Remember? We were meeting him at the restaurant. Are you ready?" She looked back at Whitey. "I'm sorry we have to leave so abruptly or I'd ask you in."

"I understand. Please apologize to your husband for me." Thanking Carly again, he shook Rachel's hand and left.

The next morning a wet nose on his cheek awakened Whitey. "Who'd have thought I could get so attached to a ball of fur," he said, petting her. "But I sure am glad you're back." Throwing the covers aside, he bounced out of bed and threw on his clothes, chuckling when he heard Nosy's "feed me" wails coming from the utility room. "I'm coming."

After pacifying Nosy, and eager to take their walk, he skipped breakfast. He knew it'd take longer than usual since John, his next door neighbor, had alerted the rest of the block the night before of Nosy's return. Their usual hour jaunt turned into three, and instead of hurrying to get back to catch up on all the work he'd put off during Nosy's disappearance, Whitey reveled in the attention they received from all they spoke to.

"I guess I'll just have to accept the fact that you're going to be spoiled," he said on their return, dropping the armload of cat treats and toys his friends had showered on them onto the table. "I've really got to get to work though, but I'm not leaving you out of my sight."

He reached for the new red leash Mrs. Smith had given them and snapped it onto her collar. Carrying her outside, he secured the leash to the wheelbarrow containing a flat of geraniums and began planting them along the front walk.

"Look who's back, Nosy." He said, when he looked up at the sound of whistling. "Hi, Carly."

"Hi," she said, running across the yard and dropping to her knees in front of Nosy, getting her face wet from the cat's nose rubbing it. "She acts better already."

"Yep. She's none the worse from her adventure. Hey, I bought some Oreo's last night. How about helping me eat some," he said, winking at her.

She giggled. "Can I feed Nosy, too?"

"Sure. You're gonna have her fattened up in no time. Why don't you give her that can of Gourmet Tuna. It's on the table."

While Whitey got their snack ready, Carly wandered into the living room after feeding the cat. Comfortably furnished but obviously lacking a woman's touch, the only personal items were the pictures of Nosy and a large framed photograph hanging on the wall. Walking over to get a better look, she saw a one-story log building with a newer, brick structure attached to it. Standing in front of it with a chef's apron and hat on was Whitey.

Mounted in the frame next to it was a faded news clipping with the heading, "Five Generation Eatery Closes Its Doors." Before she could read further Whitey came into the room with a plate of cookies. She pointed to the picture. "Is that where you work?"

He stared at it a minute. His face, so happy a minute before, broke into a scowl. "Used to. I sold it." Seeing the shock on her face at his curt reply, he softened his tone. "There was no one in the family to take it over."

"No other relatives?"

"Nope. We only had one child."

"Sounds like my family. I'm an only child, like my dad. Mom's got a sister, but she lives in Texas so we don't see her much. All my grandparents are dead."

She took an Oreo from the plate and pulled it apart. "But the three of us do lots of stuff together." Her dimples popped into view. "We're going to Cedar Point tomorrow. Dad just started a new job so he's been working a lot, but he's taking tomorrow off so we'll have the whole day together."

"What does he do?"

"He draws things." She shrugged. "He doesn't' talk about it much at home. Says it's our time together."

"Sounds like a smart man."

"He is." Her face beamed with pride.

During their visit Whitey kept an eye on the clock so Carly would get home before her parents worried. When she left two hours later she promised to visit again.

That evening Whitey had a light supper and then settled into his easy chair to watch a movie that'd been advertised as a real thriller. But he was unaware of the action bombarding across the screen, his mind on the last words Carly had said before leaving.

"Maybe you could meet my dad sometime. I know he'd like you. You like cats and so does he."

He sighed. *If only relationships were that simple.* His son, Junior, had shared his love of cats, but that hadn't held their relationship together. He tried shutting out that painful time like he'd done so many times over the years, but like a boil festering, it burst to the surface. Closing his eyes he was once again in his office at the restaurant eagerly anticipating a visit from his son.

With only a month until he graduated, Whitey assumed Junior wanted to talk about taking over the business. He pulled out the transition plan he'd worked on since the day his son turned eighteen. He could hardly contain the pride he felt knowing that "Benson's" would continue to live on.

The restaurant, just a small watering hole for locals in the immediate neighborhood when his great-great-grandfather had built it, had become so well known that people came from over sixty miles away. Never forgetting its humble beginnings, the family refused to sell to outsiders. The addition of an extra dining room was the only change they'd made, wanting to maintain their ancestor's dream of "a place to make the stomach happy and the customers our friends."

This vision had sustained them through hard economic times, and now his son would carry it on and pass it onto his sons one day. Although Junior had never demonstrated the culinary skills that came naturally to the rest of the family, Whitey never doubted his son's desire to take over.

When Junior walked into his office, Whitey greeted him with a bear hug. Sensing his son's hesitation at initiating the discussion, Whitey presented him with a leather bound book containing the family recipes. Instead of taking it, however, Junior announced he'd taken a job as an architect and was moving out of state.

"You can't do that," Whitey roared.

"But Dad, I – "

"I let you take what you wanted in college, but it was always understood that you'd take over here when you graduated."

"No, it was understood by you. Being an architect is all I ever wanted to do." He sighed. "This isn't the way I wanted to tell you, but you'd never listen when I tried to bring it up." He paused to collect his thoughts before appealing to him once more. "I hate to cook. And you know I can't schmooze people like you or grandpa. I'd be terrible at managing the place."

"I won't allow you to destroy what our family has built, just so you can live out some childhood fantasy."

"It's not a fantasy," he shot back. "It's always been my dream to create things."

"But "Benson's" is our heritage. It'll be your kids' heritage."

Trying a different tact, Junior said, "You know I love this place and take pride in what the family's created. But why can't I carry on our name by doing something I'm good at? Isn't that what it's all about? Leaving a mark?"

"But this is what the family's always done."

"Does that make it right?"

"Damn it, no son of mine is going to be responsible for destroying what our family has worked so hard to achieve." His fist slammed onto the desk, sending the lamp crashing to the floor. "If you walk out that door without committing to your rightful place here, you walk out of my life. I'll no longer have a son."

Disbelief, anger, and hurt registered on Junior's face. He clenched his jaw to control himself. "I'm sorry, Dad. I can't do it."

At his son's refusal, Whitey yanked the family picture from the wall and tore off the part with his son in it, throwing it in the trashcan. Without a word or glance in Junior's direction, he left the room.

Exhaling loudly, Whitey rose and walked over to the picture Carly had asked him about. A month later he'd sold "Benson's" with the stipulation that the family name not be used. A week after that he'd moved, bluntly telling his friends never to speak Junior's name in front of him again.

Every time he thought he'd gotten over the pain of that day, it took only a simple statement such as Carly's for all the resentment to bubble to the surface. And, for the first time, sorrow.

Three weeks had passed since Nosy's return, and Carly had become a daily visitor. Every afternoon at two Whitey'd go to the kitchen and begin getting their snack ready. Although Oreo's were always included, he'd often surprise her by adding homemade cookies or her favorite, chocolate almond fudge.

Their visits were like a poultice that filled the aching emptiness he'd begun feeling more and more of lately. The girl with the tight curls and dime-sized dimples had stolen a place in his heart he never thought he'd share with anyone again. Humming to himself, he removed the freshly baked apple pie from the oven and heard Nosy meow at the front door.

"Come on in, Carly," he shouted. "I've got a surprise for you."

"It smells delicious," she said, licking her lips and quickly taking her place at the table.

"I made it myself. It's an old family recipe. I used to bake it for my special customers." He set it in front of her and bowed exaggeratedly. "I think you qualify." Once he'd served it he asked about her day.

Listening to her talk and watching how her arms moved so gracefully to emphasize her words, he wondered if she'd end up being an actress or perhaps a symphony conductor. Her facial expressions and body movements mirrored the emotion in her voice and always held him captive as he imagined she would with an audience.

"Sounds like you've had a busy day. What about Franny? I haven't heard you mention her in a while."

Her face fell. "Her grandpa's visiting. She's too busy to play with me." She took another bite of the pie. "She's so lucky. He lets her do things her parents won't. And he buys her all kinds of cool stuff."

"I guess that's what grandpas are for – to spoil little girls."

"Yeah. She says he never scolds her like her parents do. Suzy and her grandpa would include me when they did stuff, but it's not the same as having your own grandpa." She paused a moment. "Were you ever a grandpa?"

"No, honey. I was never that lucky."

For several minutes they sat quietly, each with their private thoughts. Whitey peeked over to find her tugging on a curl, a habit she did whenever she was contemplating something important. He smiled to himself and waited patiently wondering what gem she'd surprise him with this time.

When she finally spoke, her voice was so soft that he had to lean closer to hear. "You could be mine." She blushed.

Even Whitey, who'd grown used to her precocious bits of wisdom, was caught off-guard. Afraid his silence would be taken as a rejection, he gulped down the lump in his throat. "I can't think of anything I'd rather be."

Jumping up in excitement, Carly bumped the table, spilling her glass of milk into his lap. Without missing a beat, Whitey said, "Don't worry. Grandpas don't scold."

That evening Whitey puttered around the house unable to keep the smile off his face. "I'm a grandfather, Nosy," he announced, stopping to pat her head. "Well, not an official one, but still, it feels good." Nosy purred in reply. Massaging her ears, he wondered, *I'll never know if I'm a real grandfather*, but quickly brushed the thought aside not wanting anything to intrude on his newfound happiness.

Whitey assumed his new role seriously. Each evening was spent planning their next special outing. He didn't know who was happier, the one getting spoiled, or the spoiler. He took delight in treating her to canoe rides on the river, sharing his favorite fishing spot, watching Disney movies, and splurging on hot fudge sundaes at the Dairy Queen. On rainy days they were content to sit at the kitchen table and gorge themselves on his homemade baked goods while passing the time talking. Only the stray thought of what he'd missed with his own family dampened his spirits.

The following Wednesday when he opened the door Carly hugged him and handed him a card. "It's an invitation to my birthday dinner next Saturday," she said before he could read it. "Instead of having a big party, I told Mom and Dad I just wanted a family cookout. That includes you, Grandpa. And you too, Nosy." She scooped the cat into her arms. "Mom's fixing my favorites: hot dogs, hamburgers, french fries, and corn on the cob. And instead of a birthday cake, I want your homemade apple pie."

"Oh, you do, do you? Well, I guess I can't disappoint the birthday girl," he said, tweaking one of her curls.

Whitey was up early the following Saturday, taking special care when preparing the apple pie. Adding a few extra sprinkles of cinnamon on the top, he put it in the oven and went into the garage. After tying a large pink bow on the handlebars of a blue and silver bike, he picked it up and loaded it in the trunk of his car.

When Whitey returned to the house he found Nosy curled up on the easy chair. He got her brush and picked her up, taking her place. Holding her on his lap, he brushed her coat until it shone. By then it was time to check on the pie. Satisfied that it was done, he removed it from the oven and set it on the rack to cool.

Deciding that there was nothing left to do, he went to the bedroom to get ready. He took extra time to tame his unmanageable hair, snipping a few stray ends that wouldn't cooperate. Then he put on the new green polo shirt and khaki pants he'd bought for the occasion.

"I don't know why I'm acting like a kid on his first job interview," he said to Nosy who'd wandered in and was perched on the lid of the toilet seat. "I guess I want to make a good impression on Carly's father."

In spite of Rachel's assurances that they were both pleased with his friendship with their daughter, he'd feel better hearing it from him, too. Taking a final check in the mirror, he went to get the pie and, calling to Nosy to follow, walked out to the car.

When he pulled into her driveway Carly was jumping up and down in excitement, holding onto pink and purple balloons with "Happy Birthday" written on them.

"Hello, birthday girl," he said, closing the car door after Nosy jumped out.

Carly, her face as pink as the balloons, ran over to them. Nosy, sensing her excitement, jumped into her arms causing her to lose her grip. She laughed as the balloons rose into the sky until they were just a speck in the distance.

Turning her attention back to Whitey, she said, "Hope you're hungry. You too, Nosy. Mom bought your favorite treats."

They followed a brick-lined walk that led around the house and through a grouping of evergreen trees before emerging into a large yard with an immaculately manicured lawn. To the right, tucked in the middle of four shade trees, was a gazebo.

Spotting a pond in the middle of the yard, Nosy squirmed out of Carly's arms and ran over to inspect it. When Whitey and Carly caught up with her, she was sitting mesmerized, her eyes zigzagging as they followed the foot-long goldfish darting among the rocks.

"Oh, oh. I don't think we'll see Nosy for awhile," Whitey said. Carly squealed when Nosy swatted at one of the fish and lost her balance, saving herself from falling in by digging her claws into the surrounding grass.

They watched her for a couple of minutes. When Whitey was satisfied that she'd learned her lesson and would refrain from anymore attempts at fishing, he walked with Carly towards the house.

The wall of glass that formed the entire back of it, and the French doors that opened onto a large patio, painted an impressive picture. Whitey saw Rachel busily setting the picnic table that stood in the center. A large gas grill stood to the right of the steps. At the other end was a grouping of wicker chairs with pale green and pink cushions and a small table with a vase of freshly cut gladiolas as the centerpiece. Lining the patio's perimeter were arrangements of grasses and ferns in brass and cedar planters.

"Hey, Mom. Look who's here."

Rachel put down the silverware and walked over to him as he stepped onto the patio.

"Hi Whitey." She took his hand. "We're glad you could come."

"I couldn't miss my granddaughter's birthday." He smiled. "Thanks for inviting me. You have a lovely home."

"Thank you. We're really enjoying it."

He held out the pie. "What would you like me to do with this?"

"Carly, would you take it inside? And tell your dad Whitey's here."

Once Carly was out of earshot Rachel said, "It means a lot to Carly to have you here. She said her birthday wouldn't be complete without her grandpa. Coming from such a small family, it's been hard for her, not having grandparents like her other friends do. Jake and I want to thank you for – did I say something wrong?" she asked noticing his puzzled look.

"Your husband's name is Jake?" She nodded. "What a coincidence. It's mine, too."

"I never realized that. Carly always calls you Whitey – or Grandpa now. I guess she's got two Jakes to love now."

Her kind words immediately made Whitey feel welcome.

"Why don't I see what's taking them so long." Excusing herself, she went inside.

While Whitey waited, he went over to the railing by the steps to get a better view of the pond. He was relieved to see that Nosy had tired of her game and was quietly sunning herself.

"Well, I think we're finally ready to start cooking." Whitey turned at Rachel's announcement to see a tall, broad-shouldered man, a plate of hamburgers in his hand, step outside. "Darling," Rachel said, putting her hand on her husband's arm, "I'd like you to meet – "

"Junior."

"Dad." The plate of hamburgers shattered as they hit the patio.

Reacting by reflex, Whitey spun around to leave and caught his foot on the leg of the gas grill. He stumbled and grabbed the railing, angrily jerking Jake's hand away. Still in shock, he clumsily made his way down the steps. He could hear them shouting, but the roaring of blood in his ears made it seem miles away.

Like a smoker conditioned to reach for a cigarette when the phone rings, his resentment had returned at the sight of his son. He ignored Carly's cries, wanting only to distance himself from the person that had caused the painful memories to surface once again.

"Nosy, come on," he shouted, taking long strides across the yard. "We don't belong here."

The cat perked her ears up at the urgency in his voice and ran towards him. He leaned over in mid stride to scoop her up, like a football player recovering a fumble, but she side stepped him and ran over to the trio that were now standing a short distance away.

"Nosy, get over here." Whitey kept his eyes trained on his cat, ignoring Carly's pleas to stay.

"Meow," she replied, sitting her rump on Carly's feet.

"Nosy, I mean it. We've got to go. Come here. NOW!"

"YEEEOWWLL!"

Unsure what to do, but not wanting to show any weakness by coming closer, he stood with his hands on his hips and glared at her.

"Are you my dad's father?"

Startled by Carly's question, his eyes jumped over to her before he abruptly nodded.

"Then that makes you my grandpa. My honest to goodness *real* grandpa." Her faced beamed at the revelation, but she frowned a moment later. "Then why do you want to leave?"

"Ask your dad," he said, locking stares with Jake for the first time in twelve years.

The silence was palpable as both men stubbornly refused to be the first to speak. Carly tugged impatiently on her father's shirt. "What's wrong? What did we do?"

He slowly took his eyes off his father's and looked down to see tears forming in his daughter's. He touched her cheek. "You didn't do anything, sweetie. He's upset with me." He looked over at Whitey. "He thinks I let him down. He – "

"You did," Whitey said.

Jake clenched his teeth. "I see you're just as stubborn as ever."

"MMMEEEEEOOOOOOOWWW. CCchhhhuuuurrrrrrPPPP. Mmmmmmmmeeuuuuueeerrrr." Over and over Nosy wailed at them in her alien tongue, giving no one a chance to continue the argument.

Suddenly a blur of white and gray flashed by Whitey and stopped in back of him. She squatted down and a second later pushed herself off the ground towards his back. The impact knocked him forward a few steps. Bouncing off of him, she sprinted over to Jake and repeated her actions. So agile and quick were her movements that Whitey and Jake found themselves within a few feet of each other before she finally stopped.

Then, beginning her odd wailing again, she went to stand between them, turning her head back and forth as she delivered her lecture to each of them. They stood transfixed watching the irate cat, even when she finally stopped her piercing sermon. Shooting a glance at Whitey, she walked over to Jake, and stood on her hind legs, patting his knee until he leaned over and put his hand out. She rubbed her face against it before licking it. Just as before, she repeated the process with Whitey before returning to her place between them.

Like a sleepwalker just awakening from a bad excursion, Whitey shook his head and felt the last remnants of anger evaporate. He looked at Jake and then pointed to Nosy. "Do you think she's trying to tell us something?"

Jake cautiously took a step forward. "Dad, I – "

"No." Jake retreated a step when Whitey raised his hand. Realizing his son had taken his action as rejection, he quickly added, "No. I'm the one that was wrong." He smiled as the burden of twelve years of baggage vanished by those simple words. He walked over until he was within arm's reach of his son. "I've been a stubborn old fool. I let my stupid pride destroy the very thing I was trying to hold onto."

"But I hurt you. Bad. I never meant to."

Whitey brushed the comment away with a wave of his hand. "I know that. I guess I always knew it. Just too stubborn to admit it until now." He extended his hand. "I'm sorry, Son."

Jake grasped it tightly. "Me, too, Dad." Simultaneously they grabbed each other and hugged tightly.

"MEOW." Both men released their hold to look down at Nosy, and Whitey held out his arms for her to jump into. He laughed as Nosy kissed him.

"Does this mean you're happy now?"

"Meow. Chhirrrpp."

"I guess we owe this furry thing a huge thanks for what she did," Jake said, reaching over to pet her.

"I know exactly what she'd like," Carly said, wiggling between them. "A big juicy hamburger sprinkled with tuna treats."

After the laughter died down, Carly took her grandfather's hand firmly in hers and reached for her father's with the other. With Nosy leading the way and Rachel walking next to Jake, her arm around his waist, they started walking to the house.

"This is the best birthday I ever had," Carly said, her dimples in full bloom.

The Purrfect Choice

Billy squirmed in the seat next to his father, watching the houses rush by. "How much farther, Dad?"

Laughing, his father replied, "A couple more blocks. Relax. Mrs. Cook said she still had three left."

"I know, but I want the best one." His face flushed with excitement. "I can pick the one I want, right?"

"You bet. It's your birthday, so you get to choose." His father laid his hand on his son's legs to stop their wiggling. "Tell me, just what are you looking for?"

"Well…" His father watched his eight-year-old lick his lips in concentration, a habit he'd adopted as a toddler. "I don't' care if it's a boy or a girl, but it has to like to play. And run. And chase things. You know, it's gotta be tough."

"So you don't want a cuddly lap cat?"

Billy scrunched up his nose like he'd smelled something repulsive. "No. That's no fun. I want one with spunk. I even brought some toys to check them out with."

"Well, we're here." His father turned into the driveway of a red brick ranch house. "Let's see if there's one that passes your test."

Billy had his seatbelt off and the door opened as soon as the car coasted to a stop.

"Hey, slow down, Son. You've got time." He chuckled as Billy ran ahead to ring the doorbell.

By the time he'd joined him on the front porch, a sprightly woman in her early sixties had opened the door.

"Hello, I'm Jill Cook. You must be Tom."

"Yes. And this is Billy."

"Well, it's nice to meet you, Billy," Jill said.

"Where are the kittens?" Billy said, ignoring her hand and looking past her into the room.

"Billy." Tom's face reddened in embarrassment.

Jill laughed it off. "I can see someone's anxious. Follow me, young man. They're waiting for you."

Billy almost stepped on her heels in his eagerness to follow her down the hall and into a large laundry room.

"Hold on, partner," Tom said, putting his hand on Billy's shoulder to stop him from running over to the box that contained a Seal Point Siamese cat and her three kittens. "You don't want to startle them. Why don't you wait until the momma cat says it's OK."

To curb his restless energy, Billy fidgeted back and forth on the balls of his feet exhaling quick snorts of air like a racehorse waiting for the starter's gun to go off. "Oh, Daddy, look at them," Billy said, watching the tiny creatures squirm and shove over and around each other in an effort to snuggle against their mother who was lying placidly, eyes half shut, oblivious to the excitement her brood was creating. Jill quietly spoke to the older cat before taking the three kittens and placing them on the floor.

She motioned for Billy to come over. "Shana says it's OK to meet her babies."

Looking at his father who gave him a quick nod, Billy raced over and sat down. For a second he just watched them as if memorizing their differences to tell them apart. They all had the distinct milk chocolate coloring on their legs, faces, and tails, but their coats were each a varying shade of cream, ranging from ivory to light fawn.

The largest of the three waddled over to him. "He's so soft," he said, petting its silky hair and giggling when it let out a squeaky meow. Taking a small, plastic ball from his pocket, he rolled it across the linoleum and squealed in delight as two of the kittens pounced on it, tumbling over each other as they fought for possession. The third scurried behind the washer.

"I don't want that one. He's a scaredy-cat."

"I see you're a man who has specific tastes," Jill said. "We'll just put him back."

"What's that one doing here?" Billy pointed to a black kitten curled up in the corner of the box.

"Oh, that's just a stray that was dropped off yesterday."

"It sure looks like it's been neglected," Tom said.

The kitten raised its head and yawned. Stretching to a standing position, it looked like a feline scarecrow, its fur sticking out at odd angles.

"We think whoever left it knew that Shana had a litter recently and might be willing to nurse it." She moved closer to Tom and lowered her voice. "We're taking it to the vet's today to put it down. The poor thing is blind." The ringing of the phone interrupted their conversation, and she excused herself to answer it.

Before Tom could stop him, Billy had picked up the blind kitten and placed it on the floor. It stood motionless, its head titled at an angle. At the sound of the squeaky toy the other kittens were chewing on, its ears perked up, and it began walking unsteadily, like a disoriented drunk, in their direction. When it bumped into the corner of the dryer it froze in mid stride. Instinctively, it arched its back. Its opaque bluish-black eyes stared vacantly.

"I think they want to play with you," Tom said, urging Billy away from the orphan by motioning to the two Siamese kittens chewing on his son's shoelaces.

Tom joined in his son's laughter as Billy chased them around the room on his hands and knees. When he stopped to catch his breath, they used his body as a jungle gym, running between his arms and legs and climbing up his pants before sliding back down his arms. Minutes later, losing interest in their game, they scampered over to the ball again. Billy started to roll over.

"Stop," his father yelled. Billy froze and looked down to where his father was pointing. The black kitten sat directly in his path, unaware of the danger.

"Hey, you better watch where you're going," Billy said, picking it up. Studying it for a minute, he asked, "What's wrong with its eyes?"

"I'm afraid it's blind," Tom said, walking over. "Here, let me take it so it won't get in the way."

"No." Grabbing the skinny creature with one hand, he turned away from his father and set it in the corner nearest to him. "You'll be safe here. You can stop shaking," he said, caressing its back.

"Billy. You need to leave that one alone so you can decide which of these you want. We've taken up enough of Mrs. Cook's time."

Returning to the other kittens, he tossed a catnip mouse onto the floor and watched their reactions. "That one's a fighter. Did you see how it pounced on the larger one to get the mouse?"

"I sure did," Tom agreed. "Is that the one you want?"

"I'm still deciding." Moving to the opposite side of the room, he glanced over and discovered the blind kitten had wandered a few feet from the corner. It sat motionless except for its ears that were moving like radar antennas in the direction of any noise.

"Forget that one," Tom said firmly. "Come on and decide. Which of the Siamese do you want?"

"I just have one more test for them." He knelt on the floor and explained. "I want to see which one's the fastest." He clapped his hands and called to them. "Come here, guys. Come 'ere." The baby Seal Points looked like two comedians performing a slapstick routine as they jumped, tripped and zigzagged their way to Billy.

Even the blind kitten had ventured to the middle of the floor and was now looking blankly in Billy's direction.

"OK, Billy. I think you've had enough time to decide between these two," Tom said, trying to keep the impatience out of his voice. "Which one's it going to be?"

The boy's face reflected his seriousness as he carefully studied each kitten one final time. A satisfied smile crept across his face as he reached his decision.

"Well, Dad, I wanted this one," he said, pointing over to the smaller one, "cuz he's so feisty."

Tom smiled as he walked over to him. "I think you made a good choice. I'll gather up the toys so you can hold him. Then we'll go find –"

"But I changed my mind. I want this one." He flattened himself on the floor and in a quiet but firm voice began calling to the black kitten. "Come here, boy." His voice guided the little waif towards him. When it hesitated, Billy coaxed it forward again.

"What?" In surprise and dismay his father blurted, "But it's blind."

"So? It's not his fault. When Grandma died you told me God must have had a reason. Well," he said, shrugging his shoulders, "He must have a reason for making this kitty blind."

"But you've always wanted a Siamese."

"Well...I did. But I want this one instead," he said, his eyes never leaving the kitten who was tenuously but steadily making progress over to him.

"I'm sorry, Son, but we can't possibly take it."

"Why not?" Billy sat up and crossed his arms in defiance.

"A blind cat would be a lot of extra work. Remember, Mom and I agreed you could have a kitten as long as you took responsibility for its care."

Just then the object of their disagreement finished its dark journey, stopping when it brushed against Billy's knee. "That's the way. You did good. See, Dad, it's gotta be awfully smart...and brave, to find his way to me."

"I said no."

Billy stopped petting it, puzzled at his father's stubbornness. "But, Dad, I'll—"

"No." Tom cut him off. Calming down, he said, "Besides, Billy, it could never run, or chase the toys, or do all the things you said your kitten had to be able to do."

"So I'll help it. Just like you said I should when Johnny lost his arm in that car accident. Remember how angry you got at us kids when we made fun of him and wouldn't play with him?"

The kitten let out a plaintive meow followed by a quick pat to Billy's knee. Cupping his hand under its bottom, Billy drew it to his chest and gently ran his hand down its back.

"Purr. Puuuuuuurrrrr."

With the kitten snuggled against him, the son looked at his father. "You told me it's when people are at their weakest that we should love them the most."

The only sound as Tom stared at the pair was the steady purring of contentment. His eyes misted. "I'll go tell Mrs. Cook."

"He's going to be a great friend." Billy's eyes sparkled. "Thanks, Dad."

Ruffling Billy's hair, his father said, "No, Son, I'm the one that should thank you."

The Cat's Pledge

You may think because I walk on four paws instead of two feet, have a tail, and I'm covered with a blanket of fur, that you and I have nothing in common.

But like the homeless, I, too, need shelter from the cutting cold, relentless rain, and swirling snow.

My belly growls just as loudly as yours does when it's empty, and my thirst needs to be quenched to survive.

Although not the same as yours, I need medical care to prevent disease and to heal injuries.

My fears can also be calmed with a soothing touch and a gentle voice.

Sometimes perceived as an independent loner, nothing is more satisfying to me at times than to curl up on a lap for companionship.

At nighttime, when darkness multiplies my loneliness, I crave the security of a warm body to snuggle against just as you do.

I also need protection from bullies and seek an open mind when my actions don't agree with what others may want.

When meeting someone new, I ask only to be greeted without any preconceived notions, as you would hope to be welcomed, too.

And when my life draws to a close, but before the final darkness descends, it's comforting to feel a last, lingering caress and kind words telling me that my existence meant something to someone.

In return, I pledge to shower you with unconditional love, steadfast loyalty, and unwavering companionship.

In truth, we're not so different at all.

Printed in the United States
30381LVS00005B/295-366

9 781413 758412